"The protagonist was wonderfully drawn and surprising, in that she was kind of a frumpy, sturdy woman, with a very interesting background, and lots of interesting thoughts about it. Sharon was able to weave Hattie's inner life into the outer episodic narrative. The writing encouraged me to keep rooting for Hattie, even as she was thrust into almost untenable situations."

Bill Worth, *professional editor, and author of Outwitting Multiple Sclerosis: How Forgiveness Helped Me Heal My Brain By Changing My Mind; House of the Sun: A Metaphysical Novel of Maui, and The Hidden Life of Jesus Christ: A Memoir.*

"A murder mystery with an endearing main character."
Paula Rogala, CFP®

"Made me laugh and cry all in one chapter!"
Kathy Scorse

"...mystery within a mystery."
Elizabeth Onyeabor, *#1 Best Selling Author of From the Shadows: A Journey of Self-Discovery and Renewal. Enugu, Nigeria.*

"Proverbial good read with interesting characters that challenge you to figure out just where they fit. Things aren't always what they appear to be. Sometimes like a thrill ride that takes over for the scary part. Does keep you wondering what's next and when and what are the next."
Gary N. Wodder, Ph.D. *University of Scranton. Moscow, Pennsylvania*

"Hattie—quirky, passionate, and lovable!"
Timothy C. Smith *Civil Engineer*

"Meet Hattie Crumford, a 60-something kind-hearted eccentric who shows up for work one morning and suddenly finds herself making a police report about a dead man who has gone missing from her office, and a whispered warning that masks an international conspiracy of huge proportion.

As Hattie innocently follows her natural talent for snooping, she suddenly finds herself in a struggle for life and death that leaves the reader stunned and turning the pages to find out what happens next.

Set in the vibrant neighborhoods of New Orleans, this book has it all – despair, humor, joy and intrigue. Lochman has created characters that are at once mundane and extraordinary, embroiling them in a mystery that starts small but

becomes unimaginable in scope. The prose is at once fast-moving and lyrical, revealing keen insights into the human heart. The reader is left wanting more of the unlikely duo of Hattie Crumford and Detective Hugo Gabby as they continue their search for **The Man With The Sand Dollar Face***."*
- **Ernestine B. Colombo***, author of Returning Souls: A NOVEL*

MAN *WITH THE* SAND DOLLAR FACE

by

Sharon CassanoLochman

Paperback ISBN: 978-1-62747-181-7
eBook ISBN: 978-1-62747-187-9

To my beloved Timothy Charles Smith

Thank you for following my circling thoughts and imagination into the heart of the Crescent City, across paper, and through life.

Acknowledgements

I would like to thank those closest to my heart, Tim Smith and Tim Cassano, whose love, encouragement, and support helped me to stretch my wings and take flight. To them I am forever grateful for holding my hand until I was ready to fly.

Thank you to final readers Tim Smith, Nancy Atherton, Dixon Van Winkle, Kathy Scorse, Gary Wodder, Ernie Colombo, Elizabeth Onyeabor, and Paula Rogala for accepting the daunting task of reading through a nearly finished manuscript and offering words of encouragement, insights, and reviews. Greatly appreciated was your help to spit-and-polish every last word and phrase.

To editors Tom Bird, Idony, J.R. Angelella, and Bill Worth, I am grateful for the timely influence on the structure and style of my manuscript as I eased away from the creative aspects of writing towards the equally important presentation of a finished work.

For my early readers Tim Cassano, Lisa Norman, Andrea Page, Vicki Rawlins, Suzanne Singer, and Evelyn Foreman, special thanks for looking beyond the rough draft and offering words of encouragement as I teetered on new ground.

Special thanks to Tom Bird, Sabrina Fritts, John Hodgkinson, and my friends from our special writing groups for our spiritual connection, words of encouragement, and teatime support. Blessings to all of you.

Thank you Tom Bird for giving me those blasted writing assignments and forcing me to face my fears. Thank you for your compassion and constant encouragement. Thank you for *seeing* the bigger picture and looking beyond every dot and dash to the heart and soul of my story.

To friends Sam Attardo and Nancy Atherton, thank you for feeding me throughout my writing retreat weekend, for the writer's satchel to carry my most cherished papers and pens, and for the tenderly written notes with words of encouragement that saw me through the toughest moments.

Special thanks for Ernie Colombo and Suzanne Singer for our special connections that go beyond this place into another.

For my publicist Denise Cassino, you are a teacher beyond books and a friend across miles. Thank you for designing my book cover and helping to get my project off the ground.

I am grateful for all of you and your efforts sending me off on my way onto another life journey. You are a gift and deeply cherished.

To the City of New Orleans, thank you for your diversity of sight and sound, smells and tastes.

With warm regards,

Sharon CassanoLochman

Chapter 1

Everything has a time and place, as my mother used to say.

Right now, my place was behind the antique desk on the eighth floor of the Eldridge Building in the heart of the Crescent City. At sixty-two years-of-age, I was widowed, gainfully employed at the office of Wallace C. Woodard, Private Investigator, and, for the first time in my life, I was *on my own*. But, this Monday morning I was running a bit late.

It was 8 A.M., and my clothes already clung to my skin. I pulled the limp collar of my blouse away from my neck. Puddles from the early morning rain rose like a mist of steam across the hot pavement. The pedestrian sign flashed. An impatient cabbie skirted around me as I stepped onto the curb. I smiled. Monday mornings were no longer lost in the shuffle of the mundane. I savored change and the morning chaos.

Automobile exhaust laced with the aroma of sugar from the praline shop hung heavy in the air. I stepped next to a man sprawled across the sidewalk, his back against a light pole. A tattered duffle bag and my grand-mother's handmade quilt were all that separated him from the uneven pavement. His thin canvas shoes were worn through at the toe, but the laces were neatly tied. His wild, coffee-colored hair framed his high cheeks and bearded face. Deep scars ran like streetcar tracks across his right cheek. Although in his late twenties, his face bore witness to a long life on the streets, his once broken nose slightly twisted, his eyes dark, but full of life.

"You've moved," I said.

"Changed light poles, yesterday," he said, smiling.

"How's the view?" I asked, scanning the multiple lanes of traffic and buildings that lined the sidewalk's edge.

"Better than the other corner."

"How are you today, Charlie?" I asked.

"Good, Miss Hattie, except for this unforgiving pavement," he said, rubbing his hip.

I reached into my purse and opened my wallet, weighing the twenty-dollar bill against a handful of quarters and a bus pass. I handed him the twenty.

He blocked it with his hands, forcing it back in my direction.

"How's the writing going?" I asked, pushing the twenty back in his direction.

"I've cornered the villain," he said, patting a sun-bleached notebook, its rippled pages peeking out from beneath his duffle bag. He played with the bill for a moment before tucking it into his shirt pocket.

"I can't wait to read it. Let me know when you're ready for me to type it."

"Could be a while. The villain might escape," he whispered and winked. He adjusted the stub of a pencil in the crook of his ear.

"I'll talk to Rudy," I said. "He might have a connection with someone at another building."

"You're late," Charlie said, pointing to the clock in front of a bank. He gave me a two-finger salute goodbye.

Freshly pressed professionals, unaffected by heat and humility, marched quickly to the tick of their watches around Charlie and his newly claimed corner. I wondered if their contemptuous attitude was gratitude in disguise for not sharing Charlie's space on the uneven sidewalk. I walked away, appalled at the attitude of the masses. They shared buses, streetcars, and taxis. They shared restaurants and hotel linens. They shared drinks and polluted air. They shared everything yet shared nothing at all.

I hurried the remainder of the block to my office, trying to quiet the slap-and-drag of my loose pumps against the sidewalk. The old shoes, like me, had stretched in size. I remembered the day I bought them, hoping to don an air of sophistication should I attend the opening of a Royal Street art exhibit. The shoes were now little more than the separation between the sidewalk and me and hardly aired sophistication. I spotted Rudy and waved. Two men bumped me from behind, unceremoniously knocking me to my knees.

"You okay, Hattie?" asked Rudy, our building's door attendant. He helped steady me to my feet.

I nodded and watched as the two men disappeared into my office building. "Very rude, even for a Monday

3

morning," I stated, noting a silk-screened peace symbol on the back of one of their shirts. Not very peaceful behavior.

Rudy gathered my rolling quarters as I gathered the remainder of my dignity.

"How's your wife?" I asked.

"Under the weather," he said, reopening the massive door for the impatients checking their watches, and sending messages from their phones.

"Sorry to hear that," I said. "Give her my best."

"I'll be sure to do that."

"I need to ask a favor of you for our Charlie," I said.

"Shoot."

"He is going to need a literary agent when he finishes his book. Be nice to see him earn some money and settle into a place of his own." I placed my right hand on my heart.

"I'll ask around," said Rudy, pointing to a row of shuttered windows along the top of the office building. "You've got company this morning."

I glanced up and mouthed a quick *thank you*, before sandwiching myself on the elevator between the impatients' fancy-suited shoulders, aftershave, and coiffed hairdos.

Stepping off the elevator, I shuffled down the long corridor of the eighth floor, passing private businesses and a doctor's office, trying unsuccessfully to quiet my cursed shoes as much as possible. The receptionists at the doctor's office stopped their morning chatter, replacing it with dirty looks. I smiled and nodded a good morning to them. My cheeks burned with embarrassment.

"Can't she find a different pair of shoes?" asked the receptionist with blonde hair. She slammed her iced coffee with whipped cream and pink sprinkles down on the desk and bolted from her seat. She shut the door.

I continued clomping down the remainder of the hall, approaching a middle-aged man pacing back and forth in front of my frosted-glass door.

I was not the least surprised to find the door still locked. Mr. Woodard was rarely in the office, let alone in the office early. That's why he hired me. My job was to answer the phone and take detailed messages. Mr. Woodard wasn't the kind of investigator who got real hot cases, you know, like murders and things of that nature. His job was to catch high society's cheating spouses through a telephoto lens. I wondered if anyone was trying to catch Mr. Woodard. Between his wife and girlfriend, he hardly had a moment to call his own. It was a little challenging when I first began work here, not knowing who the wife was and who was the girlfriend. I almost learned the hard way when I assumed I was talking to the girlfriend and almost called the wife by the girlfriend's name—or *was* it the girlfriend that I assumed was the wife? Lilly and Pauline. I had a hard time keeping their names and their places straight. When you work for a private investigator, you learn not to give out any information or call anyone by name—especially Lilly and Pauline.

"I need to see the private eye," said the man, barely allowing me the space to unlock the door. He smelled of tobacco and last night's alcohol. A muted tie hung unevenly around his open collar. His face was flushed and unshaven.

"Is he expecting you?" I asked.

"No, but I need to talk to him." His words raced. "Right now," he shouted.

Everything has a time and a place, I thought. I didn't think this was *his* time or place.

"I'm not sure when he'll be in." I fumbled with the key. The man nearly shared the back of my pumps as he pressed into the office behind me. He took control of the door, closing the two of us into the abbreviated space of heavy wooden paneling sodden with old pipe smoke.

His jaw clenched as his head twitched involuntarily. Sweat beaded across his upper lip. His damp shirt clung to his chest. He ran his fingers through his sparse hair and held the palm of his hand to his forehead. "I need to see him right away!" he said, shaking a fisted paper at me.

My heart pounded. I held a breath and reminded myself to stay calm!

"Have a seat, please." I motioned to the chair near the window. "Or, if you'd like to leave your name and number, I can have Mr. Woodard give you a call back as soon as he gets in," I said in the calmest manner I could muster. I felt the need to run. My mind raced for safe passage out of the office.

"Can't wait." He pushed past the chair to the window. The man stretched his neck and removed his tie. "I'll have to come back," he said. His fingers turned white as he clenched the small paper. He dropped to his knees.

He coughed and sputtered before landing face first on the floor.

I darted from my desk and rolled him onto his back. His face was purple. I tried to make sense of the situation. It was like watching a black-and-white movie. My imagination ran wild. I scanned the man's body for an injury.

"I'm going for help," I yelled.

His lips moved, but sound failed to escape. He clenched his fisted hand near his chest.

"I have to go for help!" I rose from my knees.

"No time," he muttered, grabbing my arm and pulling me toward the floor.

I cradled his head in my lap and leaned in close as he mouthed the words again through shallow breath.

"No...time. Man with the sand dollar face...."

"What?" I asked, clasping his collar. "Who?"

His head fell back, his eyes closed.

"Help, help!" I screamed, jumping to my feet. I kicked my near-dead shoes across the room and sprinted down the hall to the doctor's office.

Chapter 2

"He was right here!" I pointed to the floor with rigid indignation. "He died in my lap," I said, my tone unwavering as I defended the unraveled reality.

"Madam," a detective finally said, "dead bodies don't just get up and walk away." His face was void of expression. My cheeks burned.

A uniformed police officer forced his way through the cacophony of disgruntled EMT and police personnel slowly dissolving from my office into the hallway. I strained to listen over the multiple conversations and complaints going on at the same time.

"Nothing," one officer reported.

The detective whispered a few words in return before waving the officer off.

"I don't understand," I continued. "He was dead." I shook my head in disbelief and stared at the oak flooring. I felt like a fool. I pulled my sweat-soaked blouse from my back. There was something about this old building; the air was perpetually sticky and stale. The melee of live bodies in the cramped area did not help either. This was not the time for a hot flash; my body felt like it was on fire, from the inside out.

Do not get me started on the topic of hot flashes. Just add that to the growing list of *things your mother never told you*. Like growing a mustache, for one. There's a little tidbit to weave into a children's story. Explain it to the children while they're small so it won't be such a shock when they're older and they accidentally walk into the bathroom and catch their grandmother shaving her face. Let the little ones rock on Meemaw's lap, listening to the real story about the old witch that lived in the gingerbread house. That witch would not be luring children into a fire. Heck, the witch wouldn't have a fire—not with all the blasted hot flashes. She'd have the windows wide open. And with all the whiskers popping up along her upper lip and under her chin the children wouldn't come near her. Yes, the *real* story of the old witch. Maybe the witch was just misunderstood. Maybe she was longing for a refreshing sweet tea, hairless upper lip, companionship, and relief from the mundane.

The detective ushered the last uniformed officer from the room. A wave of muted conversations echoed along the hallway as the group reassembled down the hall at the elevator. I thought about the spunky receptionists at the doctor's office and wondered what they were thinking of me now. I wondered if they had arrogantly shut their door to the police officers as they had done for me this morning or if they were now straining to hear something about the nut down the hall. My eyes settled on my sad pumps in a pile in the corner. It was time to replace them with sneakers.

I continued to pace the office floor, motioning to the area where the man had been with an open hand. I made eye contact with the detective. "Right there!" I said. "I saw it with my own eyes."

"Passed out perhaps," said the detective, strutting his way to the window. He stretched his neck for a sidewalk view of some street commotion. I could only imagine the bottleneck of halted traffic, police cars, and onlookers. I thought of Charlie, probably forced to relocate to another light pole.

"I can't believe this is happening," I stated. I folded my arms and released another exaggerated sigh.

"How long were you gone?" asked the detective. He pinched the bridge of his nose and closed his eyes. His wrinkled cotton shirt was unbuttoned at the neck, and the tucking had pulled at the waist.

"I ran to the doctor's office down the hall to find someone to do CPR. The doctor followed me back to the office, and the body was *gone*. I couldn't have been more than just a few moments," I said.

"And do you mean a few moments like seconds or a few moments like minutes?" he asked.

I had done little more than bear witness to a situation, and now I was stumbling to defend myself. I skirted to my desk and fell into the comfort of my chair. I closed my eyes and cradled my face in the cool of my palms, blanketing my throbbing eyes.

"I don't know. Just a few moments."

"And did he say anything?" asked the detective.

"Well, he was quite annoyed, being called away from a patient." I lifted my face from my hands.

"He mentioned that one of his girls had called 911," I said, and, oh, there was the pulsating throb behind my eyes again.

"I meant *the man on the floor*," said the detective. "Did *he* say anything?"

"He whispered something about a man with the sand dollar face." I leaned across my desk toward the detective. "He said it twice. To me. Right there. On the floor." Strange as they were, the man's last words were completely outdone by his disappearing body.

"A man with the sand dollar face," repeated the detective. He scratched at a palm-sized notebook with a pen that he tucked and untucked over his ear.

"What does that mean?" he asked. The detective stood with open hands like he was ready to catch this big package I was going to drop into his waiting arms.

My shoulders curled forward as I pressed my open hand against my breast.

"How should I know?" I said.

"You stated there was an odor of alcohol on his breath," he said, unyielding in his not-so-captivating charm.

"Yes."

"So, there is the possibility that he passed out, came to, and left the building," the detective stated rather than asked. He filed the notebook into his shirt pocket and tucked the pen over his ear.

Then it hit me.

This I understood. The detective's, all-to-familiar dead-pan demeanor, the crass undertones braided with authority. I sat upright and dropped my hands to my lap.

"A possibility, I guess." I felt like a small child caught in a lie—except I was not a small child, and this was not a lie. I hated the feeling. My mind raced for a shred of validation of my innocence. I exhaled defeat as I curled over my lap. "I'm not entirely sure of anything right now." I wanted to leave and start the day over.

"And you never got his name?" asked the detective. He leaned over the front of my desk, resting his knuckled fists on the leather desk pad.

"No." I wanted the interrogation to end. After all, the disappearing dead body had nothing to do with me. I didn't invite this drama into my Monday morning office routine.

The detective raised an eyebrow. He smelled of residual aftershave left on a shirt hangered more than once between washings. His hair was cropped around his ears, and the top was a thick mass of unruly ginger-blonde curls. "I'll make out the report that an unnamed man, whose last words were something about a man with a sand dollar face, died—but then—got up and left the office. Is that right?"

I adjusted myself in the chair and cleared my throat. I shuffled with a handful of blank desk papers and a small notepad before depositing them into an empty top drawer. "Yes, but maybe not exactly."

"How so, madam?" asked the detective. His eyes were narrow and piercing as he clenched his jaw.

"Someone must have taken the body," I stated, firmly. I was proud for having arrived at this conclusion before the detective. "That would explain everything." I refolded my arms across my chest and gave a defiant nod.

"I could explain it in a lot of different ways, but that is not one of them." A long pause passed between us before he continued. "How are you feeling?" he asked.

"Quite good, considering the morning events, of course. Kind of you to ask," I said, smiling.

"Have you been seeing a doctor for any ailments recently? Are you on any medication?"

I bolted upright with both palms forced open on the desk and met the detective's gaze. "There is nothing wrong with me. The man died, and his body disappeared. Why aren't you interviewing the other people in the building? Isn't that what detectives do?" I asked.

"You must be a big help to your boss," said the detective, lowering his chin.

"I only answer the phone," I said.

The detective stood and pulled the notepad from his pocket. He patted his shirt and pants in search of the pen. I pointed to his ear. He forced a short smile.

"Mrs. Crumford, we'll be in touch if we need anything else from you. Here's my card—in case the body shows up."

I turned the card face up.

"Detective Hugo Gabby—New Orleans Police Department, 334 Royal Street," I read aloud. "That's an interesting name. Very detective-like. You found a job that fits your name. Had you always wanted to be a police officer?"

"Madam…."

"It suits you," I interrupted.

"Glad you approve." He tucked the notebook and pen into his pocket and stepped toward the open office door.

"Well, Detective Hugo Gabby, thank you for your help," I said. "I'll look forward to your call."

"My call?"

"When new information turns up," I said. "I can be reached here or at home."

Chapter 3

Mr. Woodard brushed past my desk. His long-legged stride dwarfed the expanse from the door to his office.

Everything has a time and place.

I thought Mr. Woodard's place was somewhere else.

"You got my message?" he asked, barely pausing long enough to hear my response.

"Yes, sir, I did," I said, quickly shuffling through my desk drawer for a notepad and the neatly stacked pile of office mail. "I must say, Mr. Woodard, I am a little surprised to see you in the office today. Your voicemail message sounded as though your situation was immediate. You needn't worry about a thing."

I followed him into his office. It was a roomy space with locked filing cabinets lining the wall, two leather chairs, and an over-sized desk. "I'll manage the office with the utmost efficiency." Mr. Woodard opened and closed his desk drawers as though in search of something forgotten. I shadowed him with the notepad and pen in one hand, the weekend's mail in the other. "So, you're taking off for a few days. Lovely time of the year for an impromptu holiday." He stopped abruptly, bumping into my ample bosom and knocked the mail from my hand onto the floor. Ample—that is what I would call them, for my bosoms were ample enough to balance my ample behind. After all, one does offset the other.

Mr. Woodard paused through his rummage of the center drawer.

"Pardon me," he said, too late to save the already scattered envelopes.

Mr. Woodard was a moderately handsome, yet unassuming man, regardless of the humidity or situation. That's probably what made him such a successful private investigator. That and the large client base of mis-stepping husbands and wives.

I noticed that this morning, Mr. Woodard's eyes were unusually puffy and shadowed by dark circles. His mustache, as always, was neatly trimmed, almost as if each side was a perfectly groomed brow. He never sweated, even on the muggiest of days, like this one. And, he was never without his piece. I think that's what detectives call their handguns. He wears it strapped to the side of his chest. I had often wondered if it was loaded. And, if it wasn't loaded, where did he keep the ammunition? In his pocket? Private detecting may be a lucrative profession, but it must carry a certain amount of danger as well. Otherwise, why the need for a *piece*?

I gathered the mail from the floor.

"You just missed Detective Hugo Gabby," I announced, looking up at my boss over the disheveled envelopes and papers clutched to my breasts.

"What did you say?" he asked, whisking through a stack of papers. He stopped mid-motion and peered at me over the top rim of his glasses. The right side of his upper lip twitched.

"It was the craziest thing that happened this morning—just before you arrived. A man died on our office floor." I pointed through the open doorway toward the general area. "I ran to the doctor's office down the hall for help. Unfortunately, I don't know CPR. Maybe if I did know CPR Eddie would still…." My thoughts wandered for a moment.

"The man's name was Eddie?" asked Mr. Woodard. He stared at me blankly. His eyebrows pinched together, lifting his glasses up from the bridge of his nose.

"No," I said. I giggled, thinking that was a silly thing to ask. "Eddie was my husband. Edward, I should say." I handed Mr. Woodard the mail.

"Mrs. Crumford, you digress," he said, dropping the envelopes into a drawer. "Who died on my floor?"

"Died and—*disappeared*."

"Your husband died and disappeared from my floor?"

And there it was—that blank glare over the top rim of his glasses again. It was one of the most annoying things I had noticed about him—the old schoolmarm stare. I had found myself wanting, on more than one occasion, to push those glasses back up the bridge of his nose.

"Who are you talking about?" he continued.

"I can't say for sure. The man never gave his name."

Mr. Woodard crossed his arms. His face tightened. There it was again, anger and annoyance all wrapped up and tied together in a nasty little package.

Think fast, I told myself. I didn't want to say something that might aggravate the situation and cause me to lose my first and only job.

"What I meant to say was that an unknown dead person vamoosed from that very spot in our office." I pointed emphatically at the wood flooring. "He was here early this morning asking to see *you*. I explained that if you were not expecting him that he could leave his number and you would get back with him. He was already waiting at the door when I got here. I hadn't even had the chance to listen to the phone messages. Because had I had the time to listen to the messages; I would have known that you were planning to take a few days off and you would not be joining me in the office today." I stopped to take a short breath. "But, look, here you are after all." I clasped my hands together and gathered a long over-due breath.

"Mrs. Crumford, please…."

"Oh, yes. It was rather exciting, and I should say, rather frightening as well. The man was very agitated. I didn't know what to do. I tried to calm him, and I asked him to take a seat. That's when it happened."

"What happened?"

"He died. Right there. In my lap. So I hurried over to the doctor's office for someone to do CPR, and when I got back, his body was gone."

"So, he wasn't dead?"

"Why do people keep saying that? He was dead," I said, nodding my head emphatically. "His body disappeared. The detective left his card, in case you have any thoughts on the case. Do you have any idea as to whom it might have been?" I deposited myself on the sturdy red leather chair across from his desk and smoothed out my skirt. I do appreciate looking neat and tidy, and from time to time, I guess a little flashy in my flowery skirts that tightly silhouette my overly ample twelve-hour-glass frame.

"Mrs. Crumford, what are you doing?" His finger waved erratically in front of me.

"I'm getting ready for you to interview me," I said.

"Interview you?" he asked.

"Yes, I am the prime witness in the case," I said, smiling at my significance in the situation. "I thought you might want to interview *me*." I stroked an imaginary crinkle from my skirt and avoided his unfaltering glare.

"Have you told me everything that happened?"

"Yes."

"Then the interview is over," he stated, abruptly. "Save the drama for your detective novels. Just answer the phone."

I scooted forward in the chair. "But, Mr. Woodard, perhaps I should interview you! You might have pertinent information about the case. The man did come in here looking for *you*."

"There is nothing more I can add. Case closed."

"But, Mr. Woodard, you haven't even asked me anything about him. Don't you want a detailed analysis of his appearance? Perhaps he's a client," I said, shifting my gaze to the top rim of Mr. Woodard's glasses. "Or a spouse."

Mr. Woodard forced the journal shut and deposited it back into his desk drawer. "I have enough on my mind." He slammed the drawer closed and locked it with a key that he quickly deposited into his jacket pocket. "Lilly found out about Pauline," he said, rather unceremoniously.

"Oh, how…."

"Lilly found my other phone."

"Other phone?" I held onto the side of the chair.

"Yes, I had another phone. Easier that way."

Another phone, I thought. So, that's how cheaters manage to separate their lives. Two phones. Two lovers. Two lives. My cheeks burned at my ignorance. I rubbed the back of my neck as I tried to release the knotted muscles, absent-mindedly scanning Mr. Woodard's desk and the thick client folder resting on the corner. I stretched my neck to the right, but my eyes trailed back to the folder. I could not look away. I was drawn to the folder as if it were the forbidden fruit. I had never seen the client folders. Mr. Woodard was careful to keep all confidential information locked in the wall cabinets. I forced my eyes to the floor, but they drifted back to the folder. The folder had to have two inches of stacked photographs sandwiched between the manila. Who were these people? Where were they? What were they doing? What about their spouses? What were their spouses doing when all this cheating was going on?

I wrestled with the intrigue and told myself to look away. I did. I looked up and caught Mr. Woodard's unfaltering glare. His mustache twitched, ever so slightly. I felt like a slapped child caught in the act of snooping. I was frustrated with myself for my lack of professionalism. I lowered my head and folded my hands in my lap. Mr. Woodard tossed the folder to the opposite side of the desk. A restaurant napkin stained with bleeding ink and several photographs peeked from along the edge. I shifted my position in the opposite direction and forced myself to look away from the folder and all the inherent details of what resided therein.

"Why don't you take the day off," he said, his glare still fixed.

An entire Monday off. I tapped my chin with my index finger as I mentally managed the possibilities. It would be like the time changes in the spring and fall, but instead of an hour, I could claim a whole new day. Tuesday would be Monday and Monday would be a repeated Sunday.

"Re-Sunday!" I announced, smiling at my ingenuity. I almost hugged myself. What does one do with a completely new day? It would be a gift of monumental proportions, not to be wasted or taken lightly. I contemplated all the possibilities of having an extra Sunday. I always go to…I caught myself just in time and backed up on that thought. Re-Sunday or not, I am not going to church. I added an emphatic nod to that thought; even though faith is the foundation that withstands all storms. One Sunday Mass per week was quite enough.

Mr. Woodard cleared his throat and captured my attention. I imagine that was the intention.

"What about answering the phone?" I asked.

"They can leave a message."

My shoulders slumped forward. I thought my services to be of monumental importance in the day-to-day operations of the Wallace C. Woodard Private Investigation LLC. I rose from the chair and gathered my dignity. "Oh, Mr. Woodard, what do you suppose the dead man meant when he said something about a man with the sand dollar face?"

Mr. Woodard stopped mid-scatter through another drawer. "Man with the sand dollar face?" He stared at me blankly. "Let that overactive imagination of yours have the day off."

"Have a good day, Harriet."

"Yes, sir."

"Let's remember, I am the private investigator, and you answer the phone."

"You are the private investigator, and I answer the phone." I lowered my head. "Shall I shut your...."

"Please, Harriet," he interrupted.

There it was again. *Harriet*. Oh, how I had grown to hate that name. *Harriet*, proper and form-fitted, like the tight girdle I wore when I was a teen. *Harriet*, or Henrietta as my grandmother used to say, was just plain suffocating. *Hattie* was me, bohemian and girdle-free. Hattie allowed me to take my natural shape, twelve-hourglass curves splashed with vividly hued personality.

I slowly released the doorknob as not to disturb Mr. Woodard again. That's when it caught my eye. The crumbled paper caught between the leg of the chair and the wall. Where the dead man had stood right before he dropped to the floor. I picked it up and pulled the paper taut. The words *Blue Diamonds* were scrawled across the top in pencil.

Overactive imagination and detective novels, I thought. I dropped the paper into my purse as I waited for the elevator. We'll see about that.

Chapter 4

Rudy held the door open for me as I stepped through.

"Leaving already?" he asked.

"Canal Street," I said.

"What's on Canal Street?" asked Rudy.

"Jewelry stores."

"Get a bonus?"

"Following up on a lead for Mr. Woodard," I said.

"You okay, Hattie?" asked Rudy, resting his hand on my shoulder.

"I will be."

"I heard a little bit about the commotion upstairs this morning."

"Schlagle Opportunities?" a suited man interrupted, impatiently waiting for Rudy to open the door and direct him to his destination.

"Fourth floor. Left from the elevator. At the end of the hall," instructed Rudy as he ushered the man into the lobby.

I took the interruption as an opportunity to distance myself from the conversation. I didn't want to talk. I *just* wanted to walk. I wanted to head in the opposite direction this day had taken. I wanted to get lost, at least for a bit. My spirits sagged, as well as my posture, as I waved goodbye to Rudy and streamed in with the foot traffic. I checked my watch; almost eleven. At least I needn't worry about not having money for lunch today. I would be able to eat at home after I checked out a few blue diamonds.

Canal Street reminded me of an old black-and-white movie. Streetcars and buses lobbied for space between traffic while cabbies lagged along the wide multi-lane street as they vied for potential passengers.

Louteau Jewelers. The sign twinkled as much as the sparkling promises parked on the fake fingers of black velvet in the store window. The window was tiered with diamond rings and wedding bands parked on satin pillows, would-be tokens of young love's devotion.

I rubbed my naked ring finger. Eddie didn't believe in the exchange of rings. He had thought it a waste of money, nothing more than a jeweler's invention for the unsuspecting to splurge on an unnecessary bauble.

My grandmother had shuddered at the thought of her only granddaughter entering into the holy sanctuary of marriage without a ring to symbolize the heavenly union. She offered to me the wedding ring my grandfather had given to her.

I felt like an imposter.

A buzzer rang above the door as I stepped into Louteau.

A thin-nosed woman looked over her wire-framed eyeglasses. Her hair was a mass of darkly dyed curls that accentuated her age rather than masked it.

Scanning the wall behind the cash register, I noticed the Employee of the Month sign. Written in flowery calligraphy was *Claudia*.

"I was told to ask for Claudia," I said, resting my purse on the glass-topped counter.

"I'm Claudia," she said, removing her eyeglasses.

"I met a couple at a party last weekend. The man had gifted a very special diamond to his wife. I couldn't take my eyes off of it. He said he bought it here, in your store. He told me to be sure to ask for you, Claudia."

"What was your friend's name?"

"It's on the tip of my tongue. Did you ever have that happen to you? Like it just fell out of my head."

"What does he look like?"

"Fiftyish. Average complexion. Medium frame. Thinning hair."

"That doesn't ring a bell."

"Perhaps you would remember the ring."

"Unlikely, we have quite an assortment," she said, motioning to the multiple glass display cases.

"It was a blue diamond."

"Blue diamond?"

I nodded.

"You must have us confused with another store. We don't carry blue diamonds."

"Do you know who might?"

"No."

She put her glasses back on and commenced to the shifting and rearranging of the displayed rings.

After striking out at three more jewelry stores, I snaked along the upper end of Canal Street. Someone in this city knows something about my missing man.

I walked past the imposing high-rises stamped along the sidewalk's edge. Their height offered little as of character. I thought it funny that in crossing one street, it was as if I had gone to a completely different city. Unlike the Eldridge Building, these structures were massive and modern. This part of town was the Crescent City's business district, composed of the fast-moving commodity of human thought quickly delivered through computerized faux meeting rooms and messaging systems. Maybe that's why the Eldridge Building had a doorman; Rudy was the personal touch offered to draw clientele from the glass-and-mortar.

I thought about what it would be like to be Rudy, having to open the door all day for people perfectly capable of opening the door for themselves. I had tried to open the door for myself. I smiled, remembering what Rudy had said, "Now, Miss Hattie, you know that's my job. You start opening that door, and they are going to let me go when they figure out that people can pull it open for themselves. Then, what would my wife do? Me, unemployed. Besides, you're the nicest lady in the building and if there's anyone I'd like to open the door for, it is you."

So, every weekday morning and evening, Rudy safely and diligently delivered me in and out of the Eldridge Building. I felt bad about shrugging off his concern. After all, he was the only person that talked to me, except for Charlie. Oh, I made small talk with the grocery clerks, neighbors, and shop owners. But I had never made real friends. You know, like the kind you meet for Café Au Lait and beignets. For years, my days had revolved around housekeeping and Eddie's office functions with clients. I knew the other wives, but somehow they kept getting younger, and the gap grew larger as time went on. Most of the women were employed in large firms as well, and I slowly found myself sitting on the edge of conversations rather than participating in them. Oh, everyone in my office building said hello or nodded. Except for the young receptionists in the doctor's office down the hall. They don't pay attention to me unless it's to giggle or whisper behind their hands when I pass by their office.

I followed the city's reflection through the expansive street-side windows as I continued my walk. Street-cars stopped to pick up passengers. A cabbie screeched to a halt. Fisted shouts bellowed from a man who just missed the bus, and a bike rider hopped the curb, side-stepping the road and foot traffic. I inhaled a deep cleansing breath and quickly exhaled the vexation and frustrations of my morning like a cool fall breeze whisking away the odor of exhaust and sewage.

Through the windowed reflection, I could see the expanse of floors and offices in the building across the street. I wondered if there were any disappearing bodies up there today. For me, watching the reflection was completely different from facing the experience head-on. With one glance, I could feel the surge of the city's energy and the peace of the reflected clouds drifting overhead. I could watch without participation.

To me, the world was like a blender full of individuals that society pulverized into a compote of stewed oneness. Masses of bodies walking, talking, texting, calling, and climbing the same social ladder in the same hurried way. Sometimes the contents were smooth and finely mixed while other times there were clumps of individual oneness unwilling to combine with the rest of the mass. I guessed that's what I had become—a non-congealer with society. I was a clump of quirky personality floating with the rest of the population. I wondered what I would have done if I had gone to college. Maybe I would have been a philosopher or teacher. Maybe I would have been a writer contemplating the stars and the direction of the universe. Maybe a scholar seated at a high desk next to a pile of books offering breath and soul to the contents simply by reading.

When Eddie was at the office, I used to break up my afternoons by riding the streetcars. The St. Charles Green Line was my favorite. I would take a window seat and watch as the grand boulevard of spacious front yards, and gated drives of some of New Orleans' most established and privileged were no more than an arm's length away. I pretended that I lived in those neighborhoods. Sometimes, I would get off the streetcar as though I was at my normal stop. After all, life for me was like that of a child—full of imagination. I would walk a couple of blocks, carrying myself with all the glitter and poof of class. I wondered where the people of those neighborhoods had dinner, and I wished for their social calendars. I wondered what it would be like to have people calling me to arrange for tea on the veranda and dine on delicate finger sandwiches. I imagined tossing my head back in frivolous laughter with friends over the antics of our husbands and children. *Children*. The thought had escaped before I could squelch it. In those days, I rode the streetcar to the end and then back again. It had afforded me the comfort of the company of others without explanations. No explanations needed for where I was going or what I was doing. The best part—I was never alone.

I had let my driver's license expire decades ago. Driving in New Orleans was the one obstacle I never managed to overcome when I moved to the city. Fast-moving trucks, cars, and cabs that dodged in and around traffic left me short-of-breath as the world began to sway and the road pulled off kilter. I was cutoff more times than my hair. Finally, I resigned myself to the fact that my driving days were over. Eddie was happy. He could stay at the office, consumed in uninterrupted blocks of time without having to rescue me from the front seat of the car—white-knuckled and pale, shaking and cold-frozen at the wheel. Oh, I've had people try all sorts of things to coax me out of the car. I could never let go of the steering wheel. If I let go of that steering wheel, chaos would rain down on the street. I was holding the car steady. I was holding life steady. I knew it was time to hang up the keys and learn to use public transportation.

I crossed another street and filtered into the queue behind a young woman with a toddler in tow at a stopped bus. The woman was nearly half a foot taller than I, and her linen-colored silk tignon made her look even taller.

Her russet-brown skin glowed like a polished acorn. The child smelled like a fresh breeze wrapped in baby lotion.

"Good morning," I said to the mother.

"Morning," said the mother, nodding a hello.

The little girl wrapped around her mother's legs and buried her face. I ducked my head back and forth matching the baby's peek-a-boo motion. Against the mother's best intention, the child pulled off her headband and set free a soft poof of curls around her face. The toddler giggled.

"Have a good day," I said.

The woman forced a smile as she pulled the unwilling child onto the bus. I nodded to the driver and took a seat toward the back of the bus against a window. The air in the bus was as stifling as it was in my office. Some days it felt as though no amount of air conditioning could cut through the heat and humidity. I rested my head against the window seeking the cool of the glass to comfort my throbbing head. One great thing about this city, between the streetcars and the buses, I did not need to drive.

I closed my eyes and allowed myself to rock gently with the *tick-tick-tick* of the turn signal. It was like a secret code between the bus driver and passengers. *Tick-tick-tick.* Time to check what street's next. *Tick-tick-tick* as the driver waits for an opening in the traffic. *Tick-tick-tick,* lulling me to a safe place away from disappearing bodies, irritated men, and blue diamonds. *Tick-tick-tick.*

Without warning, someone pounded on the bus door, shouting, demanding to be allowed on the bus. Startled, I nearly jumped out of my skin. The driver obliged and then briskly shut the door. I almost had to stand to see what was going on. The stocky man pressed forward with a five-dollar bill, but the driver forced up his hand, blocking the fare box.

"Exact change," said the driver.

"I don't have exact change," said the man, shouting. He cocked his head to the right and systematically scanned the bus passengers. The woman with the toddler pulled the child to her lap. The man's eyes traveled to the back of the bus. I looked away.

"You're not riding *this* bus without the exact change." The bus driver reopened the door. He switched turn signals and monitored the oncoming traffic through his large side-view mirror. "You'll have to exit the bus," said the driver, motioning to the now-open door.

The stocky man turned to an elderly man in the front seat.

"Change for a five," he demanded.

I could not believe my ears. What was going on today? Had everyone in this city lost their minds? What about common courtesy and manners?

"I don't have change," the old man said.

The bus-fare bully's top lip curled. He opened and closed his fisted hand. His knuckles cracked.

"Then *you*…give me change!" he yelled to a young girl of maybe twenty. She quickly tried to oblige, rooting through her purse.

"Get off my bus," demanded the driver, pointing to the street.

"Stop bullying the passengers," I shouted.

The bus-fare bully looked my way.

"I need to be somewhere," he said, poking his tongue lightly into his cheek.

"How far are you going?" I asked.

The bully ignored my question. The girl in the second seat meekly offered a couple of quarters.

"You can't threaten the passengers," shouted the driver. "I'm calling the police if you don't get off my bus!" His glare was unwavering. "Get off!" The bus driver smacked both hands against the steering wheel.

"Why don't you take a cab?" I asked. "Or, get off the bus and get proper change. This is not the only bus."

What was wrong with me? Why couldn't I mind my own business like the rest of the passengers? I rested against the window, hoping to ease out of the situation.

The bus-fare bully extended his hand over the seat toward the young girl. Her eyes trailed to the floor as she held up two bills and mixed change. He grabbed the money and tossed the five onto her lap. She flinched and discretely dropped the five-dollar bill into her purse. She pulled sections of hair around her face.

"Exact change," said the bus-fare bully as a quarter clanked into the fare box followed by the dollar bill. He swung a closed fist in jest at the bus driver's face, missing by only inches. He backed away, pressing open hands toward the driver.

"Now drive," he ordered.

The driver inched the bus back into traffic, shaking his head as he mumbled under his breath. The bus-fare bully punched the back of the first vacant seat as he arrogantly strolled down the aisle and deposited himself in the seat directly across from me.

"Do I know you?" I asked. "You look familiar."

He didn't answer. He pinched his lips together. His tee shirt was stretched loosely at the waist and the collar band, nicked and frayed from laundering, hung open around his thick neck. His ears were small and close to his broad face, and he seemed to have too many teeth. He had small round eyes that sat close to the broad bridge of a flattened nose. He stared at me from across the aisle. I knew I had seen him before.

"Do you work in The Eldridge Building?" I whispered.

He didn't respond.

The bus-fare bully crossed one leg over the knee of the other and tapped his foot on the back of the seat. I nonchalantly ignored his continued glare. I folded my summer jacket across my lap and smoothed my flowered skirt of creases. Mismatched to some, I'm sure. Interestingly beautiful in the clashes of color and patterns to me. My body was like my canvas, and my clothes were the palette.

My thoughts drifted to my younger days when I had learned to become fearless in fashion. Eddie was color-blind, and my mother was miles away when I began designing myself. I thought it was not only an opportunity but also my obligation. I invested in a closet full of skirts swimming in bouquets of summer-colored flowers. Sometimes, when I was home waiting for Eddie, I would dress up as if I was going to an important gala; full makeup, hair tightly curled and pulled from around my face. I waited for the imagined carriage to arrive, fantasizing about the ballroom dances and fancy dinners I was to attend. Then the old cuckoo clock would chirp and remind me of the hour. I'd hurry to wash my face and don my everyday clothes. Eddie caught me once. He came home uncharacteristically early—that was an episode I wished not to repeat. I shrugged off the memory.

The bus-fare bully's stone-cold stare inched up my spine.

"Are you sure I don't know you?" I asked again. "You keep looking at me. Perhaps you know *me*? My Eddie said I had psychic abilities because I had a way of knowing things. Maybe I knew you in another life."

I chuckled to myself, thinking about the number of times I was tempted to stop at one of the psychics' tables in front of the cathedral for a reading. I wondered if they would have told me that I had psychic abilities. I imagined them helping me set up a table of my own. I thought about what I would wear and the people who would come to me for magical messages from the great beyond. I wanted to stop along that short block and chat. I wanted to know how they knew they were psychic or if they were told of their abilities as Eddie had told me. Such a funny place to find fortune-tellers, in front of a cathedral. I was half-tempted to sit for a reading to have the mysteries of my life unveiled. But then, I thought, *what would they have to offer for the mundane*? The type of casserole I would bake for dinner or the hour of my husband's evening arrival? And if I was psychic, was I in need of a reading? Still, all-in-all, if I'd had a pocket full of cash with an equal amount of courage I would have liked the experience. I wondered if they would have told me that someday a body would disappear from my office floor.

The bus-fare bully shifted in his seat but continued to stare at me. I felt uneasy and considered moving toward the front of the bus, but I didn't want to be rude; even though rudeness was not foreign to *this* man. However, it was not in *my* character to be deliberately rude. I scrambled for a reason to change my seat. I could exit and hop the next bus in fifteen minutes or so. I tried to get my bearings for the closest streetcar or safe-haven. Funny, I thought, that I should be planning a magnificent get-away, rearranging my afternoon over the considerations of another's feelings. Why did I always gravitate toward proper behavior instead of following my gut? My gut said *move to the front of the bus,* but the ingrained thumb of my mother steered me toward chatter.

That's how it was sometimes, those free-flowing thoughts escaping before better judgment had a chance to grab the reins.

"Some people have a hard time seeing past the rough exterior of others," I said.

The bus-fare bully's face was void of expression as he continued to stare.

"The type of people that walk with a chip on their shoulder because life has handed them blow after blow." I rocked gently with this last thought.

Sometimes, it takes a while to break through tough exteriors. That's how it was with Charlie. One day, I stood nearly an hour at his light pole chirping away before he would even smile. I knew there was a profoundly good man under his rough exterior. After a while, I was looking for him. I guess I was checking to make sure he had made it through another night on the street. I started packing him a lunch. Some days, especially right after Eddie died, Charlie was the only person there to listen. I've never asked him anything personal. If there's anything Charlie wanted me to know, by gosh, he would tell me. I had wished on more than one occasion that Charlie had been my boy. He would never have seen the streets. I would have encouraged him to create his dreams on his life palette of fancy-colored notebook paper. Silly of me, wishing myself to be Charlie's mother. Maybe Charlie would think differently. I had wondered where his mother was and if she had lost sleep with worries for her boy. Maybe she was dead. Maybe she left when he was small. Unimportant information, because regardless of the circumstances, Charlie was Charlie. He was deep-spirited and awake-to-life—regardless of where he slept.

I tried to look to this bus-fare bully with the same compassion I offered Charlie. Maybe he, too, was good-hearted on the interior.

"If you had come on the bus and explained your situation, people, myself included, would have been glad to offer you a quarter or two," I said. I adjusted my purse on my lap, dropping my glance to the floor of the bus. I paused for a moment and waited for a response. "There are enough good folks in this world that would be willing to help if you wouldn't push through life so hard."

I rummaged through the bottom of my purse for loose change. I scooted toward the aisle. "Here's a couple of quarters for a fresh start tomorrow." I leaned toward his seat with an open hand. "Go ahead, take them."

He didn't move. His eyes were dark and hard to read. My gut was talking, but my mind had apparently gone to lunch. Why did I always want to help? Maybe this guy didn't want my help. After all, he could get change at his next stop. He could walk, as I had done on many occasions. Maybe, I should never make assumptions about the thoughts and actions of others. Maybe that would be a good place for me to start as soon as I got myself out of this mess. My gut reaction was to withdraw my hand and quickly. But what is the proper action when the other party does not react? I opted to set the quarters on the seat next to him and bury my unease with chatter.

"There's enough here for another fare, now that you're taking public transportation. Keep a pocketful of change or buy a pass and you won't have to bully your way onto another bus. So much easier to be pleasant to the people you intersect with along your path."

I pressed against the window, distancing myself from his unyielding glare. "Why, if you hadn't bullied the elderly gentleman in the front seat, you could have sat next to him and learned all about his life and his family. So interesting to talk to people, especially the elderly. Do you like to watch people? I do. I look at couples, which is easy to do from the window of the bus, and I try to imagine their homes and how they met. I sometimes wonder if I'm having a psychic revelation or wild imagination." I waited for him to smile or offer a kind word. Instead, he rose from his seat, dropped the quarters into his pocket, and moved two rows ahead. It struck me odd that *he* hadn't required a reason to change seats. He was not in the least worried about rudeness or my opinion of him. He angled his body toward the aisle and gave me a dirty look. That's when it hit me.

The silk-screened peace symbol on the back of his shirt.

"I do remember you!" I announced. The other passengers turned in surprise. I lurched forward to grab hold of the back of the seat in front of me. "You were one of the two men that knocked me clear off my feet this morning in front of the Eldridge Building."

The bully snarled and dismissed me with a fast swipe of his hand.

"Your shirt—the peace symbol. It stood out like a bull's eye when I looked over my shoulder to see who had knocked me off my feet. Oh no, I remember. It's not every Monday morning that I am deposited to the office in such a manner. And you were in such a hurry; you didn't even notice."

This man was not Charlie. This man's eyes were clouded and dark. Then my gut kicked in full force. Sometimes, it is important and necessary to put a proper distance between yourself, and certain people.

I found my way past politeness and followed my gut to the front of the bus, setting myself next to the elderly gentleman in the front seat. I adjusted my pocketbook into the crook of my arm and readied myself to exit the bus.

Chapter 5

I crossed the narrow streets between the gaps of traffic and cut over a couple of blocks to Frenchman where the small bistros and bars were readying their outdoor tables for the early lunch crowd. The cacophony of street musicians parleying for the afternoon curbside space was an orchestration all unto itself. Instruments strummed and tooted between bouts of laughter while other musicians hustled their CDs. I brushed from my weighted shoulders the bus-fare bully, Mr. Woodard, and the disappearing body as I zigzagged across Esplanade Avenue onto Decatur.

The air smelled of barbecued Cajun chicken and roasting beef brisket. My mouth watered thinking about sausage jambalaya and fried chicken. I glanced at my watch; it was nearly noon. I opened my handbag and checked in hopes of finding some hidden money that had suddenly dropped from a secret compartment, but found nothing save for a few loose quarters. I used to keep a couple of extra dollars stashed away in my wallet. My grandmother had told me to keep money on hand. "You never know when you might need it for an emergency or new pair of shoes," she would say. I used to put the pocket change from my grocery shopping aside. I had it hidden in one of my old slippers in the back of my closet for fear Eddie would find it.

Eddie liked to manage our money as much as he liked to manage me. I don't know what he would have done if he had found my stash. Good thing I had it, too, for everything, including the house, was in his name. The three hundred and forty-six dollars and seventy-eight cents had stretched to Tallahassee and back, as it was all I had to live on while his estate was settled. I could not bring myself to ask my mother for a penny. I emptied all the cupboards, having some of the strangest meals until one-by-one all the canned goods and fresh foods were gone. I never knew true fear until that time. The kind of fear that reaches up through your gut and drops you to your knees. I was unable to figure out why Eddie had made things so difficult for me. Why hadn't he thought ahead to secure my life should something happen to him? He must have thought he could control his earthly departure as he had controlled everything else. Funny how things worked out.

Chunks of our savings were slotted to go to his family and the bare minimum to me. Punished—and the only crime of which I was guilty was saying, *I do*. I had to let it settle in my brain before I could let it go from my heart.

I had given up everything for him, our home, and our marriage. Much of my youth had been wasted in training for marriage, mastering the domestic duties of cleaning, cooking, baking, sewing, and gardening—all the sought-after qualities found in a proper young lady. The type of proper young lady that a proper young man would like to take home to meet his mother. Once married, I held firmly to my lifelong commitment to honor my husband and our sacred vows. It had become apparent to me after Eddie's death that he had spent a great deal of thought on the disillusionment of our marriage.

I stopped mid-step and covered my face with the palms of my hands, burying the hurtful memories deep inside, like one of those secret compartments I had in my purse.

Midday navigation through the French Quarter was easy, save for the delivery trucks narrowing the side streets and a few passersby. Relaxed coffee goers read the morning edition or watched the foot traffic through the opened antique windows. The massive ceiling fans in the shops and cafés *woof-woofed*, circulating the heavy air. My mouth watered for beignets heaped in powdered sugar and dipped into a steaming cup of Café Au Lait.

Eddie had treated me to my first taste of the intoxicating duo—thick New Orleans coffee sided with an order of two piping hot beignets. I had inhaled the powdered sugar on the first bite and immediately coughed out a mouthful of sugar. I laughed until I cried at the sight of powdered sugar dusted across my chest and lap. Eddie hadn't bothered to hide his frustration with the situation. I think that's why he never shared company with me again at the well-known Café. It was, however, one of my favorite places to patronize and most likely the reason for my waistline's forever expanding degree of girth. My elevation might have been capped at a stout five-foot-two-inches, but my circumference was a forever changing landscape. I had a favorite outdoor table on the sidewalk's edge that overlooked the mule-drawn carriages lined up in front of Jackson Square. Holiday times were my favorite as there would be a brisk bite to the air. I would wrap myself in a heavy jacket and favored the saxophone player's Christmas carols. Sometimes, I would catch myself singing the words, usually after noticing a head nod or a pointed finger in my direction. Funny how I can get bumped in the middle of a sidewalk, but I can't walk down the hall to my office or sing a Christmas carol without bringing some sort of attention to myself.

I lingered at the shop windows; after all, I did have the afternoon off, and I could claim this Re-Sunday as my own. Window-shopping in the French Quarter was an easy way to pass the time. There was always something different to see, and with the constant influx of tourists to the area, easy to go unnoticed. I crossed to the other side of Decatur and lingered in front of a clothing store. The shopkeeper was busy hauling racks of tee shirts and gauze dresses onto the narrow and uneven sidewalk. I nodded hello and caught a glimpse of my reflection in the shop's window.

When did I get so old? A vision of my younger self stood next to me, smiling at the colorful expanse of people and their antics; hope painted across a young and innocent face. I blinked. Reality glared back with a vengeance. I backed away from the windowed reflection. The wrinkles and pounds had crept on without notice. No bells or alarms demanding attention or celebrations for life's experiences. Cruel, I thought. Cruel of Mother Nature to attack while I was sleeping at life. I searched for some resemblance of who I used to be. Where was the twinkle of butterfly kisses from endless summer days? Where was the heart overflowing with love and a hopeful future?

I dropped my arms to my sides. Had that person ever existed? I considered the personal changes and exchanges I had made for the five years I had lived on my own. I had exchanged rules and dictations for sleep-in Saturday mornings, a job of my own, and dreams caught in the palm of my hand. The youthful Harriet was a drone following a life-long list of instructions on how to live. Programmed happiness. No, rather programmed behavior that mimicked happiness. I had not been happy.

My head and shoulders slumped forward as I considered my degree of loneliness. I had been but a shell of a person, a servant to my marriage and my husband. A marriage and a husband nothing more than fictitious entities that I had been taught to properly worship and revere. I was a mere imitation of class and polish, an imposter of sophistication. If my old pumps could speak, they would surely bear witness to my innate frump.

I smiled and offered a crisp nod of acknowledgment at the unfamiliar face of myself staring back.

"I'm glad to meet you," I said, politely. I placed my right hand against my heart, consumed in a new awareness of my inner beauty. I blushed at my tenacity for refusing to allow the masses to dictate my definition of beauty. Finally, I know who I am. I know I'm short and thick. I know I would rather squint than wear glasses. I know I turn left when the rest of the world turns right. I know these things of myself because I have seen myself through the eyes of others. With every pointed finger or rude comment masked behind a handshake or fake pleasantry, I have seen myself through the eyes of others. Harriet tried to comply. Hattie is learning not to care. I see the lonely widow desperately seeking the comforts of companionship. But, I also see a free spirit painted in floral arrangements giving a care about something other than success, social status, and money.

I am giving. I am beautiful. I am compassionate. I am a true friend to anyone willing to *see* me.

I released a long overdue sigh—the kind held in for a lifetime. I let go of all the crap and accumulation that did not belong to me. I inhaled a farewell to the barbecue shop's alluring aroma and the possibilities of fried chicken for lunch. I clutched my purse and inhaled all the sights and sounds of my beloved city.

The French Market bustled with vendors and shoppers. The Riverfront Streetcar whined faintly across the tracks in the distance. A mule-drawn carriage clopped around a corner and out of sight. I let my eyes drift over the street's activity as if I were watching over a field of dancing clover in a summer breeze. I inhaled again, taking in the city's energy and claiming my share of an imagined breeze. I drifted and swayed, caught in the moment on this gifted day.

I scanned the length of the street in both directions. The tempo had almost instantly changed as swarms of passersby rallied to the ticking away of the lunch hour. Time was an organ grinder spinning the handle faster and faster for the dancing monkeys. I wondered what stories these people could tell. Perhaps they were wayward souls caught up in the downward fluctuation of markets and big company layoffs.

I turned to watch from the windowed reflection as people hustled for empty tables, horns beeped, and the sky dappled the horizon with paint-brushed clouds. Loud profanities spewed from a bicyclist as he swiftly avoided an accident with an opening door from a parked truck. The offending truck driver shrugged his shoulders as he stepped down from the truck and planted his foot on the pavement. The biker rounded the corner at the crosswalk, forcing a young girl to hop the curb to avoid a collision. I thought of my mother. Funny that watching the street interactions and intersections would bring my thoughts to her. I licked my index finger and placed a slash on an imaginary blackboard as I chalked one up to her. Proper etiquette would dictate awareness of oneself relative to one's surroundings, thus avoiding accidents and collisions with life. I pondered that thought for a moment.

Awareness of oneself to one's surroundings.

How could any of them be aware of anything when they're looking at the ground or their cell phones? What happened to smiling and nodding good afternoon? When did this all go away? It was like my waistline and the dead man in my office.

Poof!

I blinked away the thought and rested against the corner of a shop—a proper response to the drama-filled morning.

Then, I saw him; the icy chill inched up my spine again. He was less than one block away.

The bus-fare bully.

Odd—intersecting with the peace symbol tee shirt for the third time today.

It was like a bad dream I couldn't shake off; trailing behind like the poofter tart that's accidentally slipped out. Not the offensive *fart* discharged with a resounding wallop and a deadly smell. A poofter tart—the little bit of intestinal buildup you weren't sure you had released or if someone else had let slip. Yet, rallying in the back of your mind was the confession that it was indeed you that let out one tiny little *pssst*, hopefully, unnoticed. But, it wasn't unnoticed because it trailed you through the canned pea aisle straightaway toward the produce department. That's what this was—a poofter tart trailing behind me clear across St. Peter's and onto Royal.

I bit my bottom lip. I squinted, trying to focus on the silhouetted man near the crosswalk. I opened and closed my eyes hoping it was nothing more than my vivid imagination. Why had I given in to vanity and left the glasses at home?

Not caring to intersect with the bully's bad humor again this morning, I darted into the Voodoo shop next door and pulled a hangered sweatshirt from the rack to cover my face. I hovered in the corner of the doorway and peeked over the hoodie. "It can't be him," I said aloud. I lost sight of him through the foot traffic.

I strolled through the store past a tabletop pyramid of plastic skulls to seek solace in the security of a store brimming with people. Voodoo shops were a hotspot for tourists and locals as well. I ran my fingers along the edge of glass shelving and walked to the back of the store past key chains, incense, crosses, bundled sage and sweet grass, and Voodoo paraphernalia heavily packed and tiered along the sectioned expanse of walls and shelving. I picked up a palm-sized Voodoo doll with intent and laughed as the faces of my mother and husband popped into my mind.

A woman of about my age looked up from a paperback book and smiled.

"Funny to find tourist books in a Voodoo shop," I said, motioning to the diverse selection of sightseeing guides.

"Isn't it? *Sights and Must-Does in New Orleans*," she said, displaying the cover. Her voice was heavy, like her New York City accent.

"I wonder if they recommend this shop," I said.

She laughed and continued reading.

Sometimes the most enjoyable moments of the day are the polite interactions and exchanges with strangers. I prefer to take my smiles and well wishes with me rather than leave them checked at the door. I am never too short on time to offer a smile *or* conversation.

Twelve-thirty. Checking my watch was like a nervous twitch. I can tell you throughout the history of my life the exact time of every momentous occasion or uncomfortable moment. I had wished on more than one occasion that I could just chuck the darn thing into the Mississippi. I would be better off not tied to time and my stopwatch existence. I checked it again. I slapped my hand over the watch face, determined not to check for the time for at least the next thirty minutes.

I ventured toward the front of the store, wanting to peek onto the street and check if the coast was clear. A coincidence, it had to be. Why would the bully follow *me*? My head cycled through the possibilities. I dismissed the coincidence as nothing more than a parley with my over-active imagination. My imagination served me well to keep me company, but I had no need for it now and especially today! There were enough crazy things happening completely independent of my frame of thought. Coincidence or not, I'd rather not share a street corner with the bus-fare bully!

With a swipe of the back of my hand, I pushed concerns for the bus-fare bully and disappearing bodies away from my mind and checked the time. *Darn it!* I slipped the watch into my purse and snapped the purse closed. Re-Sunday. No checking the time on Re-Sunday. There shall be no checking of the time on Re-Sunday because time does not exist on Re-Sunday.

I asked to see a pair of feathered earrings from behind the counter and engaged the clerk in small talk about the humidity and my desire for fried chicken with jambalaya and gumbo. I waved off the earrings and inched my way to the front of the store. My humor elevated as I perused the vast collection of Mardi Gras masks near the front counter.

Mardi Gras masks were salted and peppered through-out the French Quarter. I had always preferred the hand-made masks found in the specialty shops. Huge price tags to match the social status associated with the wearing of such a magnificent piece of art. How perfectly enchant-ing it must be to adorn oneself with a one-of-a-kind mask and march completely incognito through the streets. These particular masks, however, were mass-produced to fit into any size budget. I tried on another, smiling at the silli-ness of myself. I peeked through the peacock feathers for a look at myself in the mirror.

I gasped at my shared reflection as the hairs on the back of my neck rose to his heated breath. His odor, musky and rank. He pressed against my backside as he leaned over me, resting his chin on my shoulder. He smiled, pulling a half-empty liquor bottle from his pocket. I dropped the mask and bumped into his shoulder as I dashed from the store.

I dodged between people and hurdled curbs—my old pumps click-clacking against the uneven cement. I hurried past the saxophonist serenading coffee drinkers, lazily raising their cups to the end of the last rendition.

I pressed onward. He was only a half a block behind me. I cut between the mule-drawn carriages with the drivers reading their morning papers, talking amongst themselves.

"Good afternoon, Miss Hattie," shouted one of the drivers. "Not feeding carrots to our hoofed companions today?"

"Not today. Sorry, I'm in a hurry," I shouted, picking up my pace through the Square. I exited through the gates between the psychic tables, scanning over my shoulder for a sign of the bus-fare bully when I accidentally knocked over several plastic chairs.

"Excuse me," I said, quickly righting the chairs. "Excuse me," I repeated. It was all I could think to say. After all, if the woman's psychic she would know I had just carried my heart in my throat a distance of more than three blocks.

I snaked my way through the crowd past a woman selling rendered images on canvas of dark and unearthly forces. Others held cardboard signs with their rates and specialties. It was a busy lane of intersecting foot traffic. I skimmed over shoulders for a sign of the bully. I took a step curbside. Someone bumped me from behind. I turned to face my assailant, ready with a not-so-proper list of responses for being nearly knocked off my feet for the third time today. An ancient woman of mixed descent stood bent over a twisted walking stick. She clamped her hand tightly around my forearm, her eyes milky white.

"I'm sorry," I said, gently patting her hand. "I wasn't looking where I was going."

"You're in danger!" she cackled. She raised her walking stick and pressed a crooked finger toward my face. Her grip tightened. Her long fingernails pressed into my skin. She smelled of burnt sage and camphor.

Danger? I tried to pry her free of my arm.

"Beware!" she screamed, shaking her stick. "The sand dollar face!" The nearby foot traffic came to a halt.

I fell backward, finally pulling free from her grip. A gentleman steadied me to my feet. I shook my head, retreating a few more steps. How could she know? The old woman's words—a punch to my gut.

I couldn't escape. The dead man's words had followed me.

A black bird spiraled from a nearby perch, landing between us. It pecked at a half-eaten sandwich, dragging slices of meat on the sidewalk. My blood iced, chilling my fingers and racing under my skin.

I looked back into the old woman's eyes.

"The man with the sand dollar face!" she screamed again, waving the stick wildly. "You are in danger!" She gasped for breath. Someone ushered to her to a chair. I stepped back and watched as the blind woman sat rocking and repeating the mantra. "Beware of the man with the sand dollar face!"

I could barely breathe. I fanned the collar of my blouse, praying for relief. Sounds and smells became muted against the blurry backdrop of buildings and people. I opened and closed my eyes. I steadied myself against a light pole. Her eyes—milky, white eyes.

Despite the heat, I forged my way through the streets. I felt clammy, hot, and cold all at the same time. My knees felt like gelatin as I dragged myself down Royal, my pumps awkwardly leading the way. I pinched myself, wanting to wake from this nightmare, but nothing happened. What was real? What was imagined? Perhaps the man hadn't died. Maybe Detective Gabby was right all along. Maybe the man passed out and left the office on his own. Maybe the bus-fare bully wasn't following me. Maybe he was tossed off the bus right after I got off. Maybe the psychic was just that—psychic.

The blind woman must have gotten into the ramblings in my head and got a whiff of the morning's poofter tart rallying behind me. That's all it was—a poofter tart reading.

I slowed my pace and hobbled past a homeless man hunkered on the corner. The man clasped an empty bottle in one hand and the worn rope collar of a dog in the other. The dog, like his owner, was missing patches of hair and his skin sagged around his neck. The dog panted and rolled over onto his side exposing ribs and a bony hip. I crossed myself and said a prayer for the poor beast and his master. Both had been full of life in their youth. Now, they rested on the edge of society, turned out and their life upside down, living on handouts and a dirty bowl of water. I made a mental note to fill the void in my handbag with dog bones on market day.

If I could just make it the rest of the day without another incident….

53

Chapter 6

I yanked on the massive glass door and stepped into the lobby of the New Orleans Police Department on Royal Street. The lobby smelled like an old library, except for the stale cigarette smoke that lingered at the front entrance.

"Can I help you?" asked the police officer standing behind a substantial desk that ran the width of the main lobby. He shuffled a pile of loose papers.

"I'm very excited to be here," I said, running my hands along the edge of the thickly varnished counter. I smiled at the officer. "It's just as I had imagined."

"Is that right?" asked the officer. His thunderous voice rushed the lobby like an imposing ocean wave. I thought I heard the windows rattle. His eyes narrowed. He was a massive man with a complexion as rich and deep as his voice. His hair shortly cropped, and his uniform, unlike Detective Gabby's attire, crisp and clean.

"I've never been in a police station. Interesting you should sell souvenirs," I said, pointing to the racks of sweatshirts and baseball caps along the back wall. "You know, if I was tossed in the cooler, I doubt I'd want a souvenir as a remembrance of the occasion."

The officer continued to stare.

"I'm here to speak with Detective Hugo Gabby. He's expecting me. Well, perhaps not expecting me at this moment—but expecting to hear from me." There it was again, the rambling chatter. The officer exhaled impatience. *Wrap it up Harriet*, I thought. "I was in the neighborhood, and I wanted to stop in for a little chat."

The officer rested on his elbows. He clasped his hands together and smiled. "A little chat?" he asked.

"Officer Randolph…," I said, trying to make out his last name.

"Varignon," he said.

"Officer Randolph Varignon," I said, allowing the vowels and consonants to roll from my tongue. "You were bestowed with a larger-than-life name. Perhaps your mother had wished for you to be a famous orator or actor. We are often a mirrored reflection of our name; yours is a perfect example." I giggled. "And you are larger than life." I ran my index finger up and down his exaggerated height. "Detective Hugo Gabby is another example of the pairing of a name with a personality. Why I don't think there could be a better name for him. It was like he was predestined from birth to become a detective."

"Can I help you?" asked the officer. His nostrils flared. It reminded me of Mr. Woodard's lip twitch. Could it be that some people are completely unaware of their ticks and twitches?

"Detective Gabby and I are working on a case together," I said with a wink.

"Is that right?" The officer bolted upright. "Hear that guys? This young lady is working on a case with Gabby."

Laughter from the other officers echoed behind the desk.

"I'm sorry," said Officer Varignon, "I don't believe I got your name."

"Hattie Crumford. Harriet Crumford, if you're looking for my proper name. I prefer Hattie."

"Officer Martin, would you kindly escort Mrs. Crumford back to Detective Gabby's office?"

Officer Martin furrowed her eyebrows.

"No need to call Gabby," said Officer Varignon, "he's expecting her." Officer Varignon laughed and turned his attention back toward the computer screen. "They're working on a case together," he repeated as his thick fingers chicken-scratched at the computer keys.

"This way," said Officer Martin. The officer looked like she was barely out of high school. She was small in stature with hardly enough meat on her bones to hold up the thick leather holster and gun nestled against her right hip. She was naturally beautiful with an engaging smile and dimples plopped in the middle of her dark reddish-brown cheeks. The brim of her hat rested across the top of her over-sized glasses that made her look more studious than intimidating.

Turning to follow the young officer, I caught a glimpse of a shadowed silhouette at the lobby door. I had to do a double take. The familiar tee shirt and peace sign. He was back. Or, rather, had never left.

The bus-fare bully.

I fell in behind the young officer, following her down the long corridor of plaster walls and ceiling-mounted security cameras that led to an open gang room of small cubicles.

I tried to silence my pumps as I skirted around the messy room. Labeled file boxes were stacked bunker-style several tiers high. Many of the boxes shared the same label. I straightened my skirt and re-tucked the edge of my blouse at the waist.

"Detective Gabby!" I said, waving my handkerchief, as I clopped to his desk, visually inhaling the energy of the room.

Everyone's attention suddenly turned in my direction. I felt like I was about to drive on six lanes of highway again.

Detective Gabby chased a rolling pencil across his desk with a paperclip as he spoke into a phone cradled in the crook of his neck, aiming his weighted gaze at me. His pen fell from behind his ear onto a stack of papers. Detective Gabby sat with his back against the whitewashed plaster wall riddled with dried paint drips, caked in a greasy dust. Yellowed fragments of old tape stamped a footprint of where I imagined photographs and maps once hung. In my mind, I could see the distance these walls had traveled across mysterious murder cases and heinous crimes. Cases solved and abandoned.

"If only they spoke." I ran my hands along the rough plaster.

"What?" he asked, pinching the bridge of his nose.

"If these walls could talk," I said, allowing my eyes to meander across his desk. Several empty foam coffee cups lay strewn haphazardly over the top of folders. Wrinkled papers and pencils riddled with teeth marks and minus the erasers laid scattered over layers of forms and files. Off to the side were a typewriter and a three-drawer metal filing cabinet.

"What can I do for you, Mrs. Crumford?"

"I was wondering if you've uncovered any new clues in our case."

"Our case?"

"We are working the angles, wouldn't you agree?"

"I would not, Mrs. Crumford. Why don't you go home?" He tossed the paperclip to the side. It was all I could do to hold back from cleaning his desk. I wondered how he could work on top of things rather than putting them in their proper place—like a drawer or cabinet.

"When might I expect to hear from you?" I asked.

"I'll call as soon as something turns up."

"Any luck identifying the man?"

"Madam, I have very little to go on. A body, then no body. No name. No identification. Forgive me, but I'm working on cases with bodies right now."

"Shouldn't I be looking at shots?"

"Shots?" asked the detective.

"Mug shots of missing people? Underground criminals? Gang members?" I leaned closer and whispered, "I'm surprised you didn't think of it on your own." I pinched a measured inch from my index finger to my thumb. "A little disappointed."

Detective Gabby stood and leaned over the partitioned panel separating his office space from the rest of the other cubicles and snapped his fingers.

"Martin, would you please join us in my office?" he asked.

"Hugo…."

"*Please,* escort Mrs. Crumford to a room," interrupted the detective. "Make her nice and comfortable. She's going to look at shots."

"Shots, sir?" asked Officer Martin.

"Yes, Martin, shots. Mug shots. Bring her coffee," instructed Gabby.

"Tea," I interrupted.

"Any persons in particular?" asked the officer, ignoring my request.

"As many as needed." Detective Gabby slid a pencil back and forth from one hand to the other. His bottom lip protruded out and over the upper.

Officer Martin stood with her hands and mouth open. "Sir…?"

"With sugar and cream," I added.

"What was that?" asked Detective Gabby, turning his attention to me.

"I like my tea sweet. Not sweet tea, but *sweet* tea. There is a difference. It is my only vice. Isn't that a pun? Aren't you vice?" The detective ignored my question, so I continued, "I never use lemon. Preferably real cream, although I doubt the city's budget will allow for it. I read about it in the papers. I make it a point to read the papers every day. It's important to have a clear understanding of current affairs should I be invited to enter into a conversation. Anyway, it's the budget. I'm sorry the mayor is considering pay cuts and lowering the number of police officers on staff. Crazy. Has he ever been invited to your office? By the looks of all these boxes, you officers are a bit behind on your solutions."

"Solutions?" asked the detective.

"To your cases. Like mine for example," I said, smiling at Detective Gabby.

"Take her now," instructed Detective Gabby, pointing to the open door. "Run to the corner store, if you have to, and see to it that Mrs. Crumford has everything she needs."

Officer Martin escorted me to a small room with a metal table and chair.

I tapped my foot to the tick of the large wall clock. It reminded me of the clocks in my elementary school; like the ones over the chalkboard. The minute hand staggered a minute backward before jumping two minutes ahead. It was like the minute hand had to get a running start to make it to the next minute. That's how I felt— like I needed a running start to make it to the next minute. I slid off my shoes and rubbed my aching feet. I remembered my watch and was thoroughly impressed with myself for having forgotten about the darn thing in the first place. I dragged it from my purse and set it on the corner of the table. I set my purse on it, should every tick and tock monopolize the day.

I debated whether keeping track of time was a need or a luxury. After all, indigenous tribes sequestered away from society's influences do not have watches. Stranded sailors must use the stars and the sun to estimate time. The poor and homeless cannot afford watch batteries.

If awareness of hours and minutes was a luxury, why weren't the people in charge of counting time not more aware of its passing? Not the minute-to-minute ticking between messages sent and received throughout a hectic workday. The actual passing of time. The time taken for a flower to wilt. The time taken for a butterfly to emerge from a cocoon. The time taken for the sun to rise. The time taken for a broken heart to mend. The time taken for a dead man's body to vanish into thin air.

I shuffled through the contents in the bottom of my purse and pulled out the crinkled *Blue Diamonds* note. I traced over the penciled letters. Back and forth. Around the humps and through the high-backed loop of the d, landing on the s…S!

Plural.

Plural—as in more than one.

More than a handful, possibly.

Maybe a significant amount of plurals.

A wheelbarrow load of blue diamonds and a disappearing dead man. I scattered the details through my mind's eye. Nothing was adding up.

I fumbled with the crumpled paper and its implications. Would or could I be charged with concealing evidence? The thought frightened me.

Everything has a time and place.

The best place for this crumpled paper and its inherent implications was inside my purse. For all I knew, Blue Diamonds was a limousine service or a Mexican resort. Mr. Woodard could have picked it up as easily as I and tossed the darn thing into the trash. And then what? Detective Gabby wouldn't know otherwise.

Why hadn't Detective Gabby found the crumpled paper? Maybe he was as blind as I. I allowed that thought to circle for a while. I circled all the way around to my eyeglasses, surprising myself with my depth of reason. This could be my perfect defense for why I should never wear the blasted things again. Clarity of life is not what you see or don't see but the perception of reality. I nodded and snapped my fingers completely proud of my prowess of intellectual awareness. I was clear on the fact that *I hated wearing glasses* and that wearing or not wearing glasses had nothing to do with Blue Diamonds or a crumpled paper.

I've been lucky to make it thus far without having to wear the irritating implements. My mother had strong opinions of what was proper in reference to eyeglass wear. She was quick to point out passersby guilty of eyeglass fashion infractions. *Parisian whore* was her usual response. For the longest time, I was sure Louisiana had been inundated with an influx of transient prostitutes from Paris. It's no wonder I grew up in fear of the darn things. It was my mother's opinion that women wearing glasses should not wear makeup or jewelry as not to draw attention to their face. Wearers of glasses should remain plain. Who wants to be plain? Who wants to be forgotten because you have to wear glasses? Why not wear makeup if you already have to wear glasses? Aren't glasses merely a device used to enhance the quality of life? After all, aren't the eyes the camera for memories?

No matter. I've squinted my way through this life, and I'll squint my way into the next if needed. *I'm not wearing glasses.*

I shuddered at the thought that it might be time for bifocals as if plain glasses were not bad enough. I had decided long ago that crisper vision was not that important. I see the important things in life just fine, and the rest can get stuffed into a hidden purse pocket. I let *that* thought drift for a while. It circled right back and around and flailed me right in the behind with the vision of the blind woman with her haunting white eyes. I imagine she would have opted for glasses had that been an option to save her sight. Vanity pulled from the left as reason slapped sense right back into me.

I slammed my open hand on the desk. If I have to wear glasses, then I'm opting for the most bedazzled pair of bifocals available. I want rhinestones. In fact, why settle for one pair? I could have a dozen pairs. I wondered if they sold frames with flowery prints or paisley. Why aren't women's glasses decorated with dangling beads or LED lights? I would have red, white, and blue for the Fourth of July. Tie-dyed would be nice for lazy Saturday afternoons in the garden. If I had to wear eyeglasses, why not make a statement? Why not make such a big statement that other people would want to wear them even if they had perfect vision. I mean, make the blasted things more than just functional. Make them exotic. I was surely not the only one with an aversion to glasses. I wondered if there were any artists designing eyeglass frames like Mardi Gras masks. Picasso's renderings of misplaced body parts. Andrew Wyeth frames with lighthouse temples. I imagined a store with rows and rows of one-of-a-kind hand-painted eyeglass frames arranged in an eyeglass gallery; some pairs so valuable they would be auctioned off to the highest bidder. I could hear the *bang* of the gavel. "Sold! To the lady in the flower-print skirt for one-million dollars."

The door slammed shut. Officer Martin dropped a stack of loose photographs onto the desk along with a brown paper bag and a covered foam cup.

"Where's the book?" I asked.

"No book," said Officer Martin.

"In the movies...."

"We print as needed."

"How do *you* know who to print if I don't know? Inefficient to work that way and a waste of paper, if you ask me," I said.

The officer didn't answer. She just blinked.

"Can't you let me look at the computer screen or give me a book so I can see all the photos at once? These are nothing more than a cluster of wrinkled papers, hardly what I would call *freshly printed*." I pushed the pile in Officer Martin's direction.

Some pages were folded or creased; others stamped with dirty fingerprints or stained from spilled coffee. They looked like they had taken permanent residence in the police station or the trash. Some had gobs of stuck-on crumbs like a dirty placemat used under someone's lunch. That would be an interesting item for the police department to sell in their lobby gift shop, mug shot placemats.

"Gloves?" I asked, tapping the desk with my fingers. "Cotton, please." I couldn't be the only one averse to touching the soiled paper mess. No telling how long this stack of muggers, rapists, and thieves had been here.

"Cotton *gloves*?" asked Officer Martin.

"I'm allergic to latex," I said, wiping my hands clean.

"No gloves," said Officer Martin as she eased the metal door open.

"What do you use for pat-downs?" I asked. It seemed to me that the police would not *want* to touch some people *or* their belongings without gloves. "What about crime scenes?"

"Ma'am, our gloves are not for public use. Department directive."

"Have you been an officer very long?"

"Two years, ma'am."

"Have you talked to your mother today?"

"Ma'am?"

"Call her tonight and tell her I said *thank you*. She's raised a fine young woman." I smiled. She was a nice young lady. I imagined her mother was worried sick about her daughter thrust into unsavory situations. *I* was worried for her.

"I'll do that, Mrs. Crumford." She turned to go.

"Wait…," I said, extending my hand in her direction.

"Ma'am?" She cocked her head. Her brows furrowed.

"Never mind," I said, flipping another page with the hankie.

The officer turned and shut the door, firmly. Had my mother been here she would have marched Officer Martin back in here to close the door, *properly*. I imagine Officer Martin's mother would have done the same.

I settled into my seat, as uncomfortable as it was, and took charge of my duties. I flipped pages and sipped tea. I thumbed through the photographs, amazed at the variety of criminal faces. Some baby-faced, the type I would expect to help me with my groceries. I certainly would not have suspected *them* to be criminals. I rested against the back of the chair and sipped the tea. I had imagined criminals to be donned in overcoats with brimmed hats and glasses. Probably mustaches and dressed in Wingtip shoes. I laughed aloud. I had just described my father *and* Mr. Woodard!

Two-thirds of the way through the pile and I caught sight of a familiar face. It was him.

Chapter 7

With the hankie-held photograph in hand, I hurried to Detective Gabby's office. He sat cradled in a chair thumbing through a manila folder with his legs extended over the corner of his desk.

"Here, here…." I couldn't walk fast enough.

"Find your man?" he asked, taking the paper from my hankie. Detective Gabby's feet dropped to the floor. "This him?"

"The bus-fare bully."

The officer in the cubicle next to Gabby started to laugh.

"Bus-fare bully?" asked Detective Gabby.

"The man who took my quarters this morning," I explained, pulling up a chair to the detective's desk.

"He robbed you of quarters?" asked Detective Gabby.

"No, I offered them to him," I said, nodding emphatically.

Detective Gabby sat upright and tossed the manila folder to the corner of his desk. "Mrs. Crumford…."

Experience had dictated that when someone exaggerated my name on a long exhale, it was not good and usually the precursor to a lengthy lecture or a complete dismissal of conversation. I knew to start talking before Detective Gabby could finish his exhale.

"This man followed me into the Voodoo Shop," I said.

"Spend a lot of time in there?" he asked.

Laughter sprang up from the detectives scattered around the room.

"I thought I had lost him at Jackson Square when the woman with white eyes grabbed me."

"White eyes?"

"Detective Gabby," I said, "he followed me here."

"Probably after your handbag. Mickey Mullen—Mouse on the street," said the detective. "He's made the rounds in here over the years."

"Mouse, because his name is Mickey?" I asked.

"Because he's a gutter rodent," said Detective Gabby.

"Is that today's paper?" I asked, dragging the folded front page in my direction.

Detective Gabby shuffled the sections together and handed me the Times-Picayune in its entirety.

I skimmed the front page and slammed my hand down on the headlines about a missing man.

"Do you have a photograph?"

I tapped the article insistently. "Right here—New Orleans business tycoon missing for three days."

"It's not my case," said Gabby.

"Might be our man," I said.

"Mrs. Crumford, sometimes people go missing because they *want* to disappear. Officer Martin, please see Mrs. Crumford safely to the bus stop. I believe she may need a few quarters."

Chapter 8

Back at The Eldridge Building, Rudy opened the door for me with a graceful bow. It made me feel like royalty. My cheeks burned with a blush.

"You're usually headed out of the office, instead of in at this time of day," he said.

"Just stopping in for a minute. Need to tie up a few loose ends," I said.

Rudy playfully tipped his hat to me.

I like it when he does that. Rudy was not what I would call a handsome man, but there was something handsome about him. Perhaps it was his polite nature or the way his uniform remained crisp throughout the day, regardless the weather. I could only imagine the tedious efforts of his dear wife to so lovingly and laboriously attend to Rudy's well-manicured appearance, day after day. Rudy was like a whitewashed linen. Why a good wife would only put out properly washed linen on the line to dry. Laundry day was akin to hanging out your aptitude as a woman and wife. Rudy's wife could walk with her head held high; since her husband's uniform was the perfection of starch and creases.

"Glad to see your spirits up," he said, smiling.

"Was your visit to Canal Street productive?"

"Dead-end."

"Sorry to hear that."

"I'm still working on the missing body case," I whispered.

"Sounds like a movie."

"Documentary," I said.

"Any leads?" he asked.

"No," I said, shaking my head. "Did the police interview you?"

"No."

"Rudy, you see everyone that comes and goes into the building."

"Yes, ma'am."

"I'll interview you then and pass the information on to Detective Gabby."

Rudy touched the brim of his hat and nodded to a woman in heels and a fitted gray suit. She seemed to be unaffected by the humidity or her high heels. She smelled like my grandmother's flower garden. Her elongated frame was graced with sophistication. She filtered into the crowd and soon disappeared; her gray suit camouflaged amongst her peers.

I can't remember a time when a gentleman smiled at me—or nodded. The gray-suited woman was like a box of long-stemmed roses. I was more like a handful of dandelions, some in bloom, others ready to puff free in the wind. Men don't smile and nod at dandelions, only roses.

"Rudy, what can you tell me of your whereabouts this morning?"

"I was here," he said.

I recorded his response verbatim in my notebook.

"And what were you doing?"

"Opening the door."

"From what hours?"

"From 7 A.M. until now."

"You notified me that someone was waiting at the office for me, did you not?"

"I did."

"What can you tell me about the man?"

"He asked for the private detective's office," said Rudy.

"What else?"

"I told him he needed to go to the eighth floor and then I opened the door for him," said Rudy.

"Did you see the man any other time?"

"No."

"What happened when you went to lunch?"

"Garvey took over," said Rudy.

"Garvey?" I asked.

"Maintenance."

"Did you notice anything else unusual this morning?" I asked.

"Besides the EMT and police officers?"

"Did you notice anything else throughout the day?"

"Yes," said Rudy. "My wife gave me tuna instead of peanut butter and jelly." Rudy smiled, then laughed.

"This is serious, Rudy, a man may have been murdered," I said.

"You don't say."

"Where is Mr. Garvey now?"

"Probably in his basement office," said Rudy.

I closed the notebook.

"By the way, how was your tuna sandwich? I love a good tuna sandwich on toast with grapes and chopped apples. Did your wife add fruit?"

"Just tuna and mayo," he said.

I took the elevator down one flight and approached the basement office, knocking on the maintenance door. Garvey sat at a small table fashioned as a desk. Hot-water tanks and thick electrical cables lined the wall. A light fixture hung from a dusty cord. The maintenance office smelled like the basement of the church that my grandmother had dragged me to every Sunday.

"Can I help you?" he asked, rising from his chair.

"Good afternoon, Mr. Garvey. I'm Mr. Woodard's assistant. He's the private investigator on the eighth floor.

"Yep," he said, saltier than I had expected.

"I'm also working with Detective Hugo Gabby…*on a murder case*. I'd like to ask you a couple of questions."

"Not like I gotta choice. You're already here."

"Where were you today between noon and 1 P.M.?"

"Manning the front entrance, Rudy was at lunch," said Garvey.

"Did you notice anything unusual?"

"Nope, not especially," he said.

"Did the police talk with you?" I asked.

"No." Garvey pushed loose paperwork to the side of his table.

"A man died in my office this morning. We believe it to have been murder."

"Believe?" His eyes opened like saucers.

"Wouldn't the police know if someone had been murdered?" he asked.

"They would, except, the body *disappeared*."

"How did you lose a dead body?" Garvey asked.

"We didn't lose it. It disappeared. You can understand the importance of our investigation into the matter."

"Sure. You lost a dead body."

I raised my finger and pointed at him.

Garvey rubbed his hand across the bristles on his chin.

"I mean, disappeared."

"Is there another way out of the building?" I asked.

"The back stairs, but they'd still have to go out the front entrance. The back door is for emergencies and deliveries only. Besides, an alarm sounds when the back door is opened, and I'm the only one who has the key to turn off the alarm." He scooped a lanyard heavy with keys from the edge of his desk.

"And there were no alarms that went off?" I asked.

"Not today."

I tapped at my chin with the end of the pen. "Did you see anything unusual today?"

"No, the typical guys and gals. I was only at the door for the hour. Maybe Rudy saw something after we changed shifts."

"What about while you were traveling the building?" I asked.

"Traveling the building?"

"Do you do rounds?"

"Only on an as-need basis," he said. "Showing new tenants the available office spaces, checking on air conditioners, heating problems. Sometimes the ladies room on your floor gets plugged. Feminine products—even though there's signage not to flush."

"Were you out and about in the building this morning?"

"I was."

"Did you see anything unusual?" I asked.

"Do you mean besides the police and EMT?"

I cleared my throat. "Say around the hour of eight this morning? A nervous gentleman headed to the eighth floor?"

"I did see a nervous fellow on the elevator."

"What can you tell me about him? Did he say anything? Did he speak with anyone?"

"The guy was sweating a lot," said Garvey. "Although, nothing unusual for this time of year."

"Think back, Mr. Garvey. Did you notice anything else?" I asked.

"Besides the clamped paper in his hand?"

"You did see him!" I wanted to cry. I hadn't lost my mind. I was not crazy. The man had existed. The importance of the paper existed. If Detective Gabby had conducted proper detecting procedures, *he* would have been the one to find out about *Blue Diamonds,* and I wouldn't be headed to the clinker, slammer, big house, cooler, pokey, or any of the stone-cold locked-solid jailhouses for withholding evidence. The only way out of this warped mess was to solve this crime! I tried to compose myself. "That's the man, without a doubt."

"The only reason I noticed him was that he was pacing the elevator squeezing that paper until his knuckles were white," explained Garvey.

"Mr. Garvey, you have been of the utmost help."

"By the way, did the police say anything about what was on the paper?" he asked.

"They did not. Perhaps, we should keep that information between us. We wouldn't want to hamper the police investigation by leaking important details. By the way, you do a magical job maintaining all these wires and heaters and things," I said, motioning with one broad swoop of my hand.

On the eighth floor, I paused at the doorway of the doctor's office. The receptionists looked at each other and laughed.

"I need to ask you a few questions," I said. "Did you see anything unusual this morning?"

"Besides the commotion in your office?" asked the rather perky redhead. The receptionists looked at each other and laughed.

I ignored their rudeness. "I've noticed that you leave the office door ajar and I thought that perhaps you might have seen or heard something."

"Just the police," they said in unison.

"Did the police interview you?"

"They asked a few questions about you," said the blonde as she pulled at a thick strand of hair and pressed it to the corner of her mouth.

"About me?" I asked.

75

"They wanted to know how long you've worked here," said the redhead.

"A man died in my office, and his body disappeared," I said.

The redhead rolled her eyes.

"I was hoping you might shed some light on the subject," I continued.

"We've already given a statement. Close the door on your way out," said the blonde.

I passed my office door and continued down the hall to the back stairwell. I turned the antique brass handle. The steel door swung open with a creak. Eight flights down. It would be a long haul down these stairs with a dead body.

Chapter 9

I deposited the day's mail and messages on Mr. Woodard's desk. His chair beckoned me into its deep leather bucketed seat. My feet dangled like a child's on a swing. I inhaled the intoxicating aroma of the soft leather. I could get used to having my own office. I scooted forward in the chair and firmly planted my feet on the floor. What a lovely idea. The offices of Hattie Crumford and Wallace C. Woodard, Private Investigators. How positively improper. I nestled back into the chair with a confident smile and tendered the possibility of my name above Mr. Woodard's on the frosted glass. Mine should go first, of course, for alphabetical reasons.

The air conditioning vent near the side of Mr. Woodard's desk rattled, jarring me from daydreams and comfortable leather. I wondered if I would share this office and if we would need to hire someone to answer my calls. I would allow my assistant to open the mail. I would also take her out to lunch once a week. She would be more than an assistant. She would be my most trusted confidant. I would hire someone my age, of course, vetted in experience and sensibilities.

Then I wrestled with the idea of having a *gun*. I laughed aloud at the idea of a chest holster fitted like a *living bra* around my ample bosoms. Where would I buy a gun and how would I learn how to use one? Maybe I wouldn't need one. "Too dangerous," I announced in a sudden outburst. That happens a lot; my mouth moves faster than my brain. With my elbows resting on the arms of the chair, my steepled fingers tapped in rhythm with each swing of my feet. I would most definitely need a lower chair. I leaned back and gazed at the tin-plated ceiling, tarnished from age. I chuckled to myself, imagining Mr. Woodard's surprise to find me sitting in the front office, gun and private investigator's certificate parked on a leather desk pad.

Mr. Woodard was adept in sensibilities. He would see how this could only improve his business. I would take on real investigative cases and leave the matrimonial clients to him. I tapped my finger to my chin. Detective Hugo Gabby would have given my morning statement a lot more consideration if I had been a private investigator.

I parked the leathered throne behind the desk and sauntered over to Mr. Woodard's expanse of windows. The Eldridge Building was a grand example of New Orleans architecture. Ornate carvings graced the corner-stones and soffit with large arching windows wrapped in Juliet balconies. The windowpanes, stacked three-high, ran the length of the wall behind Mr. Woodard's desk. The sun was glorious as light radiated through the pared glass. I loved the imperfections of thickness and color. Sometimes, depending on the weather, the windowpanes were a sky blue hue, and other times, like today, they were crystal clear. I ran my fingertips across the uneven glass. A horn beeped below, towing me from mental slumber. I pressed my cheek against the pane and smiled. Charlie was back at the light pole.

I closed Mr. Woodard's door, defining my portion of the office. My space included a desk, two side chairs, a computer, and an antique rotary phone. Mr. Woodard must have inherited the phone with the office. I wondered what happened to all the old rotary phones. They were probably in the waste yards waiting for a call, like me. I lifted the phone from the cradle balancing the weight of it in my hand. I bet I could crack someone over the head with it and still call 9-1-1.

I sat in the comfort of formality behind my desk. Every day was an experience finding my way through the computer's windows. Thank goodness for Rudy. Mr. Woodard had assumed I was vested with a wealth of computer experience and knowledge. I must have been the last person in the world to learn how to use one. Toddlers know how to operate computers. I imagine there are people with a dog or pet monkey that can turn on a computer. The idea that I was slower than a pet monkey to learn a simple office operation was not something I wanted to advertise around Louisiana. I wondered how many people had a pet monkey. Why would someone want a pet monkey? How would you go about finding a pet monkey? I know there aren't any pet monkey stores in New Orleans. Maybe the Internet sells them. That would be a search to do. I bet I could find a pet monkey on the Internet.

The Internet. The thought took me back to my first day on the job.

"Your desk," Mr. Woodard had said, his expression void of emotion. "Pick up the mail, answer the phone, take detailed messages, and put my appointments on the calendar." He had handed me the computer passcode. Off he went for the remainder of the day, leaving me holding the computer passcode and an imaginary calendar.

I had sat for two full hours trying to find a button or switch to turn on the darned thing. Finally, I scurried down to the lobby and summoned Rudy upstairs. I told him it was an emergency. He had mumbled something about the office goofs not being able to open the door as he fell in behind me. I pointed to my desk. Rudy looked around and shrugged his shoulders. "I don't know how to turn on the computer," I said.

He stared at me like I was from outer space.

"I have never had to use one before. Can you please put me in a window? Can you come and show me how to get into the Internet? There's a calendar in there somewhere that I'm to keep."

Rudy shrugged his shoulders and gave me a disapproving look.

"Password here. Internet there. Calendar there. You'll find your way around. You can't hurt it, that's the important thing to remember. The x in the corner closes the window. Let me know when you're ready to sign off," he said, ending my speed-dial lesson.

Off he went, leaving me in a new world. I was a foreigner who didn't speak the language. I knew if I could pull this off I could do just about anything. Later, I signed up for a computer course at the library. I remember thinking I may even buy a home computer one of these days.

I drifted over the morning's events and thought of the disappearing body. If only I had insisted on getting the man's name. I thought of the religious implications for his soul. Maybe he had wanted a priest or a rabbi to pray over his body. *His body.* What happened to the body? I shuddered at the thought of a person stealing a body. What purpose would they have for stealing a body? I got up and locked the office door. I didn't like the idea of body thieves, and I didn't want to join the missing body tally.

I drummed my fingers on the desk. I could go home. I was not accountable to anyone. I stared at the frosted glass trying to imagine what it would look like to see my name in broad letters above Mr. Woodard's name. If I had been a private investigator, I could be working this case and flashing a fancy business card. I bet my natural psychic abilities would help. I would know who was being truthful and who had done the horrific crime.

I could already be at the police station lining up all the probable suspects and dazzling Detective Hugo Gabby with my detecting abilities. Possibly famous for solving: The Case of the Disappearing Body. It sounded like the title of a book. *Man with the Sand Dollar Face. The Case of the Disappearing Body, A true story by Hattie Crumford, Private Investigator.*

It would be hard to walk down the street; everyone would know my face from the millions of sold copies. I imagined my life story woven into and around an inter-national mystery. What happened to the body? The only clues were a man with a sand dollar face and *Blue Diamonds*. I could imagine it as a mini-series and wondered what actress they would get to play my part.

Waving to imaginary fans from a grand Mardi Gras float, I pretended I was tossing necklaces and maybe a few signed copies of my book to the women and children lined along the sidewalk's edge waiting for a glimpse of the famous writer. I tapped the desk. *It couldn't hurt to just look into it*, I thought. It would make a great book. It might not be too late. I am still working the case. I stretched and adjusted the phone's position while contemplating the idea. I shuffled blank notepapers. It could only be an asset to my job; like a bank teller that doubles as a Notary Public or is that *Notary Republic*? Mr. Woodard would probably be happy that I'm trying to better myself. I'm sure he would encourage me to use the office computer to research the possibilities.

I typed private eye. Nothing came up. I thought for a minute and then tried private investigator. Bingo! I jotted down the steps and resources. In the middle of the third page of notes, it hit me. I can't explain it. For some reason, it struck me funny. Not just funny, hilarious. *Private eye.* I could see Mr. Woodard's eye peeking through a keyhole, his mustache bristling against a wooden door. His glasses sliding down the bridge of his nose. Private eye or was it *Private I?* I had to think about it. I started to laugh. "Private Eye," I said, reassuring myself. It even sounded funny. I scrolled onto another article about private investigators, and I broke into a full laugh. I began to wonder if I had gone through

life thinking an eye for I? I laughed again at the silli-
ness of the whole thing. I sat back into my chair. Was it
private eye? "Private eye," I said again. I laughed so
hard I almost wet myself. I laughed down the hall, in
spite of the clank clanking of my pumps. I laughed in
spite of the receptionists in the doctor's office. I laughed
as I hurried to the ladies' room so as to not have a truly
embarrassing moment. I snorted and coughed with my
fisted hand to my mouth as I tried to squelch the ava-
lanche of laughter. I landed my rump on the toilet seat
just in time.

Chapter 10

"Do you always keep the door locked?" asked Rudy, his uniform jacket draped over his arm, and his hat atop a small pizza box.

"Not usually," I replied. I stepped back from the door extending an open hand.

"How's it going?" he asked, pulling the chair from the window to the front of my desk.

"Research for a case." I closed the computer window and pushed aside the keyboard.

"Need help?"

"Your pizza's going to get cold," I said.

What was it about the smell of hot pizza that was so intoxicating? The crust! The aroma swirled around the office like a genie let out of the bottle.

"Did you miss lunch again today?" asked Rudy.

"I'm trying to lose weight," I said in jest.

Trying to lose weight.

That phrase had consumed the better part of my adult life. I should've had it stamped across my forehead. The explanation that I am *trying* to lose weight is another way of saying that I am completely aware that I'm chubby and I am taking the appropriate action to rectify the situation.

"Help yourself," he said, sliding the pizza box in front of me. He pulled out a couple of napkins and two colas from a pocket.

"What about your wife? Won't she be expecting you for dinner?" I asked.

"She went to her mother's."

A dark cloud shadowed the office as my mother's wrath addressed the improperness of sharing a pizza with a married man.

"I—I can't," I said, stumbling over the words. "It wouldn't be proper."

"You're married."

Rudy dragged his chair behind the desk and pushed it next to mine. "Scoot over. We need to talk."

I shifted toward the wall and angled the keyboard in his direction. I had just explained why sharing a pizza would not be proper and he's moved in right next to me, pinning me between properness and a situation that had the potential to turn into a gnarled mess.

"That's just a story I tell," he said. His eyebrows furrowed as he frowned. He stared at the floor. I leaned over, trying to meet his eyes. "It's all a lie."

"Why?" I sat within the unraveling space behind my desk. I took in a deep breath and exhaled the image of my hovering mother from my mind.

He sat quietly for what seemed like an eternity.

"The people that work in this building don't care to know anything more about me than a good morning or good night."

Rudy put his hand on my shoulder. "You said more than good morning and good night. You cared enough to listen. I used to make up stories about my wife and no one in this building so much as blinked an eye—except for you. You kept me on my toes with questions."

"Well, it's time to shake off the tablecloth and peel the potatoes," I said.

Rudy's head leaned back as he quietly chuckled. He ran his hand up and down his cola can. "I was in a relationship. She left me," he said. His eyes were dark and his eyebrows furrowed. "We lived together for twelve years. She wanted more from life than a door attendant's salary. It was around that time my mother got sick, so I moved back home to care for her. I haven't dated. Who's coming home with me for a romantic evening with my seventy-six-year-old mother sharing the sofa?"

"You can still meet someone. Many people come together in their golden years. You must know people that are in their second or third marriages."

"I never thought of it like that," he said.

"But one thing is for sure; you won't meet anyone unless you stop telling people that you're married. Of all the ladies that frequent this building, the right one could be right under your nose."

"You're right about that," he said. He circled the top of the cola can with his finger.

"There's one more thing…."

"What's that?" he asked.

"May I? I'm starving."

This was the first time I had shared a meal with a man other than my husband. To say I was shocked is putting it mildly, but it's not the first time I thought I knew someone only to find out differently.

"What are you going to do?" I asked.

"Haven't had a chance to think about it. Maybe I could just say we've gone our separate ways," said Rudy.

"I don't think anyone will care one way or the other," I said.

"I wasn't going to tell you, either," he said as he passed me another slice of pizza.

I looked hard at my friend. His explanation was perfectly understandable. How much was he obligated to share about the private matters of his life with superficial acquaintances? Is there a proper amount of information to dismantle and does anyone care? Superficial relationships need not be privy to private matters. Doesn't a person have a right to a certain amount of privacy?

I was going to have to get to know Rudy all over again.

"You know something, Rudy?"

"What's that?" he asked.

"You don't know a lick about the people in this building, either. You *think* you know them, but what do you know? You know what floor they work on and the fancy letters or titles associated with their businesses. But, you only know what they want you to know."

"You have a point."

"Your perception of another person can be based on the real or imagined."

My mind wandered through the twists and turns of my life and marriage. "I bet if you changed your perception of life, you could change your reality," I announced.

"Where did that come from?" he asked.

"Sorry, it's the way my mind works. My mouth circles hither and thither around and in between my thoughts."

"I'm impressed," he said. He shifted a slice of pizza from one hand to the other.

"That I can do two things at once?" I asked.

"The gravity of the statement," said Rudy.

"For example, if I'm looking and waiting for something bad to happen, it most assuredly will. Now, did I make it happen because I was expecting it? Did I subconsciously cause an expectation to become a reality?"

Rudy stared at the ceiling. "I expected my girlfriend to leave because she kept telling me she was leaving me if I didn't get a better job. What you're saying is that I manipulated the situation which in turn caused her to leave?"

"Exactly," I said. "Did you look for another job?"

"No."

"My point."

"So, if my perception had been that she was madly in love with me and happy in our relationship, regardless of my job, then we'd still be together?"

"I believe so," I said. "But your girlfriend also has a role. She has her perception that creates her reality."

"So, how do you manage to have a happy life when the expectations become reality times two?" he asked.

"Maybe when your perception of life is happy and fulfilling, you'll attract the same type of person. You both will create a reality with similar happy thoughts."

"Key is to find someone that looks at life through rose-colored glasses."

"Key is to change your perception first. I think you'll find each other when you're both looking for the same thing." I watched Rudy chew on his pizza crust.

"Did you have tuna for lunch or was that another story?" Rudy let out a laugh. I rested my hand against his and smiled. "It's nice to meet you, Rudy."

Rudy's cheeks turned red. "Do you mind?" he asked, "Is that today's paper?"

"I swiped it from Detective Gabby," I said. "Check out the front page and pass me the horoscopes."

"What am I looking for?" he asked, holding the paper at arm's length. I guess Rudy doesn't like the idea of wearing glasses either.

"The missing business tycoon. I think he's my disappearing dead man," I explained, flipping over to the front page.

"Look him up."

"How?"

"Internet. People search."

Rudy went to work scanning the search engines. I flipped through the paper for my horoscope.

"Look at this," said Rudy, angling the computer screen in my direction.

A small window flashed with a coded password already filled in.

"Woodard—must have a prepaid account," he said.

89

I leaned over Rudy's arm and hit enter.

Rudy copied the name *Alexander Mendonhale* from the front page story. We waited, the timer circled as the search engine sifted through public and private records.

"Bingo!" shouted Rudy. "Wife, children, and address."

Rudy pressed in next to me. I tried not to move. I liked the feeling of the weight of his body as it rested against mine. Maybe Rudy wasn't aware that he was touching me. I've never had a man other than my husband touch me before. Another man has never occupied any portion of my space. *Is this what friends do?*

"Let's try for images of Mr. Mendonhale," said Rudy, waking me from the blissful moment as he tapped at the keyboard. He scrolled through the blocks of photographs.

"Any familiar?"

"No."

"Not your man then," he said, slumping into his chair.

"I haven't had a chance to tell you about what's happened today," I said.

"Besides...."

"Yes, besides the disappearing body," I interrupted. "I was followed by Mouse nearly all day."

"Mouse?"

"That's his street name."

"Why *you*?"

"Robbery, more than likely."

Rudy's knee settled next to mine. I tried to steady myself against the shared space of my knee with my dinner guest.

"You already saw him. He was one of the men that knocked me off my feet this morning."

"Wish I'd gotten a better look at him."

"One thing I don't want is a better look at the white-eyed psychic woman."

"What?"

"Do you believe in ESP?" I asked.

"Back up. White eyes?" asked Rudy. He shifted in his chair and dropped his hands into his lap.

Wait, I shouted from inside my head, I wasn't ready for you to move away from me.

"White eyes?" he asked, again. His eyebrows furrowed. His intensity was unsettling.

"You ever go to the Cathedral when the psychics are lined up and sit for a reading?" I asked.

"Can't say I have. I don't have much reason."

"I've always wanted to sit for a reading," I explained. I took a sip of cola and patted my mouth with the napkin. I wrestled to maintain normalcy while I was keenly aware of the fact that a man was nearly sitting in my lap. I hoped my nose wouldn't start running or I'd get a gob of cheese stuck between my teeth. That would be worse than a bloody hot flash right now. I pressed the napkin to my lap.

"Hattie, white eyes?" he asked.

"Blind, but the woman sees everything," I said, nodding empathically.

Rudy closed the empty pizza box and shoved it aside.

"She sees everything," I repeated.

"Blind."

"Blind," I said.

"Hattie, this conversation is exhausting."

"She sees—you know, other things in other ways. How else could you explain it?"

"Explain what?" he asked.

"*Beware of the sand dollar face*," I said, mocking her rant.

"You're joking."

"Perfectly serious."

There he sat, just like Detective Gabby, with his hands open like he was waiting to catch a big package that was falling from the sky. His mouth opened but he failed to speak.

"Rudy," I said, "Those were the last words."

"Last words?" he asked before closing his mouth.

"The disappearing dead man's words. The man with the…," I said, stopping mid-sentence. The doorknob turned, slowly. I pointed at the door. I half expected to see Mr. Woodard or Detective Gabby. The office door inched open, and a thin-faced man with sparse hair and bulging eyes stepped into the office. I felt pinched between the man's sharp odor of stale cigarette smoke and Rudy's aftershave.

"Can I help you?" I asked.

"Robert Boudreau?" he asked with the hint of a Creole accent. His eyes darted back and forth from me to Rudy.

"Wrong office," shouted Rudy. The man cleared his throat as he retreated a step back, half-bowing before snapping the door closed. "That was odd. No one in this building with that name. Keep that door locked when Woodard is out of town."

"Maybe he's meeting someone," I said.

"Well, the name is on the door," stated Rudy. He tossed his crumpled napkin onto the desk.

"Sometimes people don't take the time to read."

"Besides, the building is closed," said Rudy, ignoring my explanation.

"Maybe someone let him in."

"Still feels odd," said Rudy. He retrieved the napkin and tossed it into the wastebasket. "I'll give you a ride home. You've had enough excitement for one day."

"Too bad for his affliction," I said.

"Affliction?" Rudy cocked his head.

"Must have been a war hero. He had a metal hand."

Chapter 11

"Hardly the war hero type," said Rudy.

"We shouldn't make assumptions," I said. "All he did was accidentally open the wrong door."

"Something's just not sitting right with me," said Rudy. "Come on, let's get you home."

I closed up the computer while Rudy gathered the accumulated trash from our impromptu dinner. "Thanks again for dinner. I'll bring in lunch tomorrow," I said.

"Sounds like a plan," said Rudy.

Sounds like a plan, I thought. That was the same as a yes. Not an eloquent acquiescence but a man's way of wholeheartedly accepting an invitation in a plain, general speaking way. Rudy's way of saying *he'd love to have lunch with me tomorrow*.

"Since Mr. Woodard is away for a couple of days, we can eat at my desk." I spit out the words before my brain could catch up. Properness in a variety of compartments flushed through my mind. What was I thinking? "We can invite Charlie," I said, regaining equilibrium. I smiled at my ingenuity. Three for lunch would most definitely be a more proper setting, especially in my office.

"Something other than peanut butter and jelly?" he asked.

"I thought you had tuna today."

He shook his head. "Made that up, too. Seriously, you kept me on my toes."

Getting to know Rudy was going to be like baking a cake from scratch. I shrugged my shoulders. I like to bake.

I flipped the light on in Mr. Woodard's office to do a quick look-over before locking up. The desk was tidier than usual. I thought about the folder. Why didn't I just look away? Mr. Woodard should never trust me alone with a client folder. Who knows to what depths I would travel through photos and notes if left to my own devices. I could imagine my mother's hasty flight down from heaven—snatching the folder from my hands and dragging me back to my desk by my hair.

Rudy leaned in around my shoulder to steal a peek of Mr. Woodard's office. I could feel his muscular frame against my back. He smelled good. I love the subtle fragrance of aftershave. I didn't want to move. Rudy skirted around me to the window for a sidewalk view. I could picture my mother and Eddie as they tried to trip and shove Rudy back out into the hallway, slamming the door shut behind him, locking it with *my* key. I looked up to the ceiling and glared. *Can you just let me enjoy this moment?*

"Looks different than street side," said Rudy.

"That's what Charlie says about changing corners." I joined him at the window. "I've never seen it from here at night." I looked for the time, but my watch was gone. I let out a heavy sigh.

"What's wrong?" asked Rudy.

"My watch."

"Broken band?"

"I must have left it on the table at the police station. I'll stop in tomorrow and check their lost and found."

"They have a lost and found?" asked Rudy.

"They should. They have a gift shop," I said.

Rudy raised an eyebrow. "No kidding." He circled Mr. Woodard's desk. "Nice office."

"I know. I'm thinking of becoming a partner." Rudy's response was laughter. I rubbed the heel of my palm along my upper arm. I wanted to take it all back. The disappearing body, white eyes, that statement, and tomorrow's lunch. On second thought, not the lunch, but everything else.

"In what capacity were you considering this business venture?" he asked.

I couldn't answer. I swallowed hard. "We better be going," I said.

"Hattie," said Rudy. He rested his hand on my shoulder and squeezed gently. "You took me by surprise, that's all. I didn't mean to hurt your feelings. You would make a great partner. Are you thinking to be his office manager?"

I struggled to say the words. "Private investigator." I made it this far without a lightning bolt—might as well jump in with both feet.

Rudy clenched his jaw tightly. I looked away. That *was* stupidity on my part. One hundred percent stupidity. He'll never take me seriously. Rudy gave a tender shake of my shoulder. "You would make an amazing private investigator. Why you could sneak in just about any-where."

My spirits raced. I clasped my hands together. "Those were my thoughts exactly!" I said.

"No one would suspect you in a million years," said Rudy. "Woodard's got private eye written all over him."

"You're the only person I've told," I said. My ears and cheeks burned from blush. I couldn't look him in the eye.

"It's safe with me," said Rudy.

"Mr. Woodard's got a lot of cases," I said, motion-ing toward the row of locked cabinets.

"Are those full?"

"I have no idea. They're locked."

"That one's open," said Rudy, pointing to one of the drawers.

"Where?" I asked.

"Here," said Rudy. "It's not locked all the way."

Rudy pinched the tab and gently pulled. The catch clicked open.

I knew I was teetering on the edge of losing my job. My gut was screaming w*rong, wrong, wrong!* Rudy's hand rested on the drawer. The cabinet squealed along the metal glides as Rudy rolled it open.

S*lam that sucker shut.*

Push in that lock.

Never, never, never come into this office again!

I must be having an out-of-body experience. Tempo-rary insanity. Kissing the job and the security it provided *au revoir.* I waved my hand in front of Rudy, but it was not a *stop*—what you are doing kind of a wave. It was an indecisive wave like I wanted to see in the drawer, but I would let Rudy take responsibility for opening it with this weak *poof* of a stop wave. My knees felt like rubber. Rudy paused. I placed my hand over his. I looked him squarely in the eye.

Our foreheads bumped as we both lurched forward for a sneak peek at the forbidden fruit.

There it was, a full drawer of manila folders that smelled like an old library book. There was nothing on the surface to distinguish one folder from another. No alphabetical arrangement. Nothing like the labeled boxes in Detective Gabby's office. I ran my finger over the top of tightly packed photographs to the raised edge of a displaced folder.

"It looks like the folder that was on his desk this morning." I pointed to the creased edge of a restaurant napkin.

"Let's have a look," said Rudy.

"We shouldn't. I could lose my job."

"We're not going to know any of these people. Just take a quick look. What could it hurt? You want to be an investigator. So investigate," he said.

I wanted to run and leave Rudy here alone. No telling what he would do in here by himself. He'd probably have his feet on the desk with Woodard's day calendar sprawled across his lap by the time I got back.

"This is not investigating. It's snooping," I announced.

"Let's see if you have the guts for this type of work," said Rudy. His voice was low and edgy. Rudy was egging me on.

"You're just trying out the job to see if it's right for you. Think of it as student teaching," he said.

Maybe Rudy was right. An apprentice has to start somewhere. Mr. Woodard must have had unpaid snooping escapades to sharpen his skills. I bet this was how all great investigators got started. How else is one to become better at their craft? I would merely be honing my skills. If I wanted to see my name on the door, then I better get honing.

We need to keep everything exactly as it is otherwise Woodard's going to know." I gingerly set the contraband on the desk, and with the ever-so-slightest nudge, I teased the cover of the manila folder open.

Rudy and I stood shoulder-to-shoulder over the first photograph.

A middle-aged man at the side of a sports car, wearing fancy leather shoes and khaki pants with a short-sleeved golf shirt. He wore sunglasses. I pressed against the pile with my open hand and peeled back the corner of the top photo just enough to see the next shot. It was the same man at an outdoor café with a woman dressed in a pink sleeveless tightly-fitted dress, her hair a thick wave of curls that ran down to her lower back. The man was holding her hand. I thumbed through the pile. I thought I would throw up. "I've seen enough." I closed the folder and put it back into the drawer, leaving the lock partially depressed.

I did not have the stomach for the secret life of Harriet Crumford. I doubted I would be able to continue working for Mr. Woodard. How could I face him? I was going to have to come clean. I decided that, in the future, it would be in my best interest to avoid this type of adventure with Rudy. I would continue to answer the phone until Mr. Woodard's return, but not as gloriously as before.

Move over Mouse.

My photograph might be joining yours with the jailhouse computer printouts.

Chapter 12

I marched to the office with all the force and gala of a Mardi Gras parade with three packed lunches carefully tucked and toted in a large shopping bag. I had considered making the sandwiches last night, but proper protocol dictated that my first luncheon party sandwiches should be as fresh and inviting as spring flowers. With yesterday's dissipated theatrics mildly dispersed through last night's restless slumber, I was grateful for my Tuesday morning routine. I found Charlie on the corner and could see Rudy graciously opening and closing the lobby door a half block away.

Thank goodness, the Voodoo magic was gone.

Hello mundane.

Charlie looked different today. His hair was combed, his cheeks a rosy pink. My grandmother's quilt lay neatly folded next to his backpack.

"Would you like to join Rudy and me for lunch today, Charlie?" I asked, patting the side of the stuffed bag. "Tuna and fresh fruit."

"Sorry, Miss Hattie, I would love to, but I have an appointment."

I waited for a moment, allowing the space of time for clarification. Instead, Charlie played me with a pretend pout. I squeezed his shoulder. I loved Charlie and was glad to see him happy. There was no need to know anything about his appointment. He was happy. That made me happy.

"Perhaps tomorrow," I said, handing him two sandwiches wrapped in foil and pink ribbon, a glossy red apple, and a pastry.

Charlie deflected the food with an open hand.

I circumvented his reach and dumped the items in his lap. "It'll spoil." I nodded a goodbye and hobbled in the old shoes toward my building, my feet still sore from yesterday's hike across town.

"You're here bright and early," said Rudy as he tipped his hat to me.

I felt like a queen entering her palace.

"I've had an epiphany!" I announced.

"An epiphany, sounds serious," said Rudy.

"I am going to be the best receptionist this side of the Mississippi," I said as my purse drifted slowly down my shoulder.

"Well then, give it your all," said Rudy as he opened the door.

"Lunch," I said, motioning to the bag. "Noon?"

"It's a date," he said.

It's a date? Did he mean—date? Or a luncheon date of friends gathered on this particular day. Surely, his intentions were friends-only in nature. How does one know the difference? I took a deep breath and held up a finger.

"It's just a saying, Hattie," said Rudy. His face was stern and his eyebrows furrowed. He graciously opened the door and with his other hand ushered me into the lobby.

I glanced over my shoulder to Rudy.

He winked and smiled.

I waved—at least I think I waved. I can't be sure, as a thick fog of unknowingness enveloped my head. I felt the rumblings of emotions I hadn't felt for decades.

I almost skipped the length of the eighth floor. At this moment, nothing seemed to matter. I had nearly forgotten the reasons for all the tossing and turning last night. Gone was the mental image of a dead body, white eyes, and Mouse. I tucked our lunch into an empty drawer and imagined Rudy sharing my side of the desk at noon. Unfortunately, I hadn't had time to pick flowers from my garden.

I settled into my seat and listened to the computer hum, booting up. The answering machine blinked. I readied my pen and pad for messages. Two messages and three hang-ups. The first message was from Mr. Woodard with a brief explanation for a Friday cancellation. Friday's meeting was not even on the calendar; he must have deleted it himself. I listened to the second message three times. Mr. Woodard's wife, Lilly, had left a detailed message ripe with expletives of where he could go to find his belongings. I checked the time. The call came in after eleven last night. Woodard's call was at nine-thirty. I tapped my pen on the notepad.

Pauline?

I contemplated my obligations, as my only office duty was to take messages and to manage Mr. Woodard's calendar. I dialed his cell phone. His line was dead.

Detective Gabby's words circled in my head. People either disappear because of foul play or because they do not want to be found.

"Pauline," I said.

Chapter 13

Mr. Woodard had told me to bring a book to the office, if I was so inclined, as the phone calls would be few and spaced at length. I never brought the book. It wasn't because I don't like to read. Reading is my favorite pastime. I believe that it's my moral duty to read. Reading a book is like offering a breath of life to a character—but for fear of my mother bolting from her grave in a swirling cloud of condemnation, time on the clock remains just that.

My mother organized life into compartments. Properness being the largest compartment of all. She decreed me to be proper, inwardly and outwardly, even if unhappily, proper. I believe that in her mind it was her God-ordained duty to call out anything less than proper. I learned at an early age to live according to my mother's standards or be doomed to suffer for eternity. My life's purpose was to exist on the edge of society with a forever smile pasted on a blank face, speak when spoken to, and never harbor an opinion of my own. The political policies of home, marriage, and society were to be the regurgitation of the men in my life like my husband or father or even Mr. Woodard. I envy any woman with a voice. I don't care if she's speaking the gospel, politics, or fiscal changes—as long as she's speaking freely.

For the duration of my marriage, I had properly skirted my way around the house and yard; prints and colors my only diversity in palette. I was always ready for the immediate attention of a cup of coffee with a neighbor or a friend—*none of which came*. The fear of engaging my mother's disapproval kept me properly in my place and properly dressed.

Where was my mother last night?

I shuddered at the thought of unlocked filing cabinets and manila folders flopping opening in plain view of unwitting eyes. Well, maybe not so innocent eyes. I blinked, trying to free myself of the vision of the couple holding hands in the photograph.

Then, a doubly serious lightning bolt of self-awareness smacked right onto the top of my head.

Life is a series of concessions.

At that moment, I conceded to owning up to my flaws and apparently snooping was one of them. The best thing to do with a weakness was to turn it into a strength. Private investigating could be my ticket to the pearly gates.

Chapter 14

My desk drawer opened and closed more times than the revolving doors at a bank. I'm not sure exactly where I thought the sandwiches would go. Maybe it was for the pleasant waft of the sweet smell of pastry. Sugar—it was like my senses were in tune with the sweet stuff. What could be better than a landscaped kitchen counter of manicured cupcakes, cakes, and finger pastries? I'd wager against anyone to show me something better than sugar. Sugar defied all the laws of nature. It could change its disguise from caramel to cotton candy, sweet tea to lollipops, ice cream to powdered beignets. It could be poured, scooped, licked, chewed, and smelled two blocks away. My mouth watered at the thought.

As the morning ticked away, the tension mounted. I was "doing" lunch. I half chuckled at the thought. I couldn't contain myself. This morning could not go by fast enough. I circled the office, stepping ever-so-lightly so as not to disturb the lilies of the valley nestled in the sweet grasses of my imagination. I was no longer in the private investigating office of Wallace C. Woodard but in a make-believe kingdom where wishes come true. I danced the wastebasket to the other side of the room. I hummed, completely absorbed in managing every square inch of luncheon space. I wondered where Rudy might sit. I squared the chair under the window. He can decide. I shoved the computer monitor to the edge of the desk and wiped away the parked dust. My grandmother must have trembled in her grave from the pure horror of my office linens.

I was managing my first luncheon *date*. How much longer? I checked my wrist for the time. Blast! Maybe I had misplaced it for a reason. I wrestled my chair into place and sat properly waiting for the minute hand on the wall clock to tick. I wondered how much time I'd wasted in my life looking at the time. I was addicted to time as much as I was addicted to sugar.

I dotingly arranged the delicate pink bows and ribbon on the foiled sandwich packages. Lunch with a friend should be an adventure. More than tuna with fruit on twelve-grain bread. A meal prepared for a friend should be a wrapped token of affection, a serious endeavor to create a palette of colors and flavors and the tastiest treat. I wanted my first luncheon party to be memorable. I'd been waiting for years for this occasion. If only I lived closer to the office. How much better it would have been for us to eat in the shaded area of my backyard surrounded by my flower garden. I could have picked a bouquet, not so large as to interfere with softly spoken conversation, but a bouquet large enough to dapple the table with color and fragrance. Gentle droppings of flower petals would salt and pepper my starched tablecloth. We could laugh at our private investigating prowess and share invented stories about the outdoor café couple's escapades. I inhaled the possibilities.

Chapter 15

I watched as the bundled bag of miserably unopened luncheon sandwiches and sweets sank between the damp and crumpled paper towels to the bottom of the bathroom trashcan. My chest heaved from repressed waves of stuttered sobs as the bows and ribbons hit bottom. The smell of the pastry sickened me. My stupidity sickened me. I hugged the sides of the sink before running to the toilet to vomit.

I rinsed my mouth of the foul taste of lost expectations, wiped my hands clean of the situation, and left the ladies' room and all the imagined possibilities in the trash. I cradled myself down the hall, past the receptionists, past this moment and into the next. I slowly closed the door and fell into my chair. I would quit. Stay home. I hugged myself and rocked over my lap. I could do a lot of things, but I would never be able to forget.

Rudy—a no-show.

A hasty conversation with Garvey at the front door after waiting for nearly two hours, only to reveal that Rudy had gone to lunch with a couple of friends. I felt like a forlorn teenager stood up for a date.

My mind waged war over the indignity of the situation. I tossed and turned at what I might have done wrong. Was I too pushy? Was it my misunderstanding of his comment this morning? Was it me and all of my baggage? Was it my weight? My height? My looks? My age? My ignorance?

Tears dripped onto my lap. I didn't have the strength to wipe them away. I didn't have the strength to finish the day. No longer would this job carry the same meaning. No longer would I look forward to arrivals and departures. No longer would I ever wish to speak freely and openly to another person. I cradled my face in my hands and rocked. I felt violated and exposed. No longer did I wish for companionship. I clenched my fist and slammed it on the desk. How could I be so stupid? So stupid as to believe Rudy and I might be *more* than friends.

I rested my head on the back of my chair and stared at the ceiling. I thought of the gray-suited woman that passed us on the street yesterday. That's what Rudy wanted for a friend. Not me. Oh, and to think of what I was dreaming. I tried to squelch the sobs. I had allowed myself to imagine *possibilities*.

There are no possibilities for a person like me.

I rocked in the chair, soothing my soul. I patted the hankie under my eyes. I didn't even care to see Charlie.

Chapter 16

"Mr. Woodard? I've been trying to reach you all day. Your wife…." My head was spinning.

His response was rapid and to the point. I could barely hear him over the phone.

"A disk? What folder? Where?" I asked.

His words were quick and whispered.

"You'll find me, *where*?" I asked.

He hung up.

I redialed his number.

"What do you want me to do with it?" *Click*, the line disconnected. I tried again. Silence. Mr. Woodard needed a folder.

Second cabinet from the right. Top drawer. Third folder from the back. Have Garvey drill open the cabinet lock.

I burst into Mr. Woodard's office and ran to the filing cabinets. I almost tripped over my own feet. I repeated his instructions. "The second cabinet from the right, top drawer, third folder from the back."

Then it hit me. Square in the face with all my improprieties.

I'd already had this drawer open.

I exhaled a long breath as I gently tugged at the drawer pull. The lock clicked almost flush with the cabinet. I exhaled. That was close.

How did Rudy open it last night? I couldn't get enough of a grasp to pull it out. I dumped the contents of my purse onto the desk swiping loose change and a tube of lipstick to the side. I slapped the purse onto the desk.

I needed tools.

I high-tailed it to the elevator.

"Garvey!"

Chapter 17

I wiped my clammy hands on my handkerchief and tried again. I set the small pliers around the metal tab and tugged. The tab popped open. I curled my fingers around the drawer handle and slowly opened the drawer. There it was again, the forbidden fruit sandwiched between the manila. I hovered over the drawer thinking of last night's adventure with Rudy.

My head dropped as my ego slithered to the floor. I felt dirty and defiled. I had allowed his leg to rest against mine. I wanted to creep back into bed, pulling the sheets up over my head, never to leave the house again. Why did I allow him to drive me home?

How would I ever face him, knowing he simply had a better offer? Left for lunch with friends. I staggered at the thought. I thought *we* were friends.

I thought we were—possibly more.

My emotions rocked and rolled. A couple of old buddies show up, and he forgets about our momentous luncheon plans. Then he's a no-show after lunch. Goes to show how little I know Rudy. He's not the prompt and predictable door attendant any longer.

Who is he, anyway? Where's the Rudy I thought I knew? Probably still dining on savored conversations with gray-suited, long-stemmed women and his friends.

I will never allow him to see the girth of my hurt.

I drummed my fingers on the side of the cabinet drawer. My face burned as my emotions swaggered from hurt to anger. I grabbed the drawer with both hands as a sense of the situation settled in, followed by red-hot rage.

I knew the true definition of the problem. Rudy *was* married. It was the only explanation. That whole woe-is-me story was nothing more than a fabrication. I kept him on his toes, all right. He thought he was going to wine and dine me with hot pizza and cold cola. What did he want from me anyway? Money? Amusement? Yes! Amusement. That's all I was to him. Maybe pity. Give the old bird a little attention to make her day. But the game took an unexpected twist with the misunderstanding at the front door this morning. Charades were over. It wasn't fun any longer. The amusement had dissipated into a mess of stringy hot mozzarella.

My cheeks burned. I fanned myself with the handkerchief. He's a cheater. *I can't share a pizza because you're married.* Poof! Suddenly single. I slapped my forehead. He's probably got two phones like Mr. Woodard. That was one tall tale he had spun last night. I should have known better. I slammed my fist down on the top of the cabinet. With a final swoop of my hand, I pushed the whole sorry situation out of my way, but it rolled back around. The hurt. The innocent rambling thoughts of a garden lunch. The death of a friendship—no! The grief for the loss of an anticipated friendship.

I brought my clenched fist to my mouth. I wanted to cry and scream and run. I allowed my head to rest on the top of the cabinet. The cold metal felt good against my forehead. I wanted to climb in and lock the drawer. I jammed my hankie in the folder's spot and slammed the drawer shut just as the phone rang.

Chapter 18

Teetering over my desk, I managed to grab the phone before the call forwarded to voicemail. It was Mr. Woodard. I was glad he had called back. His voice was low and his words barely discernible.

"Take the disk with me—but not in my purse," I repeated.

"And where *are* you, Mr. Woodard?" I asked, struggling to hear his response.

"Laying low?"

What the heck does that mean? Laying low. Like someone was lurking behind him in the dark ready to choke him with a phone cord. What about my phone cord? Instinctively, I peeked around my desk and followed the cord to the wall.

"You stumbled onto what? Exchange of what?"

His words halted.

"Don't hang up!" I pleaded. "What do you know about blue diamonds?"

There. I said it. Blurted it out, right across the international phone lines for all I know.

He had hung up.

"Going away for a few days with your wife, but I know you're not with your wife. Have Garvey drill open the cabinet," I muttered under my breath, shaking a raised fist at the ceiling. "Disappearing dead bodies! Why can't the man stay on the phone long enough for me to ask a proper question? Someone should let me in on what's going on around here."

I set the folder on Mr. Woodard's desk and opened the cover minus the drama and circumstance of last night's folly with Rudy. Mr. Woodard's familiar handwriting was scrawled in a coded language across restaurant napkins and hotel stationery. I thumbed through the snippets of fast food, parking, and gas receipts tucked in an envelope. No disk. There were hundreds of photographs. I flipped through the pile one-by-one assuming they were in chronological order for a reason; starting with the photos from the café.

It was unsettling to witness the private moments of two lovers as they held hands and laughed over a glass of wine. Other photos were of the same couple entering a hotel. There were photographs from inside the hotel lobby at the hotel bar. Three-quarters of the way through the stack, the couple was back at their favorite café. This time the woman had her hair arranged in soft curls on top of her head, and she wore a clingy black dress. It was like I was watching a movie. It reminded me of the professional photographer at the Mardi Gras parade last year. I had been close enough to hear the camera's click-k-k-k-k-k-k as the shutter rapid-fired one photograph after the other.

There were notes with times and dates. I could only imagine the rage and distaste a spouse would feel lumbering through the day-to-day marital discourse of their spouse. Mr. Woodard's client must be one angry spouse and someone with a lot of clout to demand this attention. Secret phone calls, drilling cabinets open, hiding the disk—but not in my purse! Where else am I going to carry it? He uncovered an exchange. Exchange of what?

I continued through the photo diary past a car ride in the country, horseback riding, casino gambling, and all the way back to the café where the man was offering a plushly covered jewelry box to the woman. Who exactly had Mr. Woodard been sent to watch? The man or the woman?

The next photo followed with the man standing over his lover closing the clasp on the gifted necklace. Rudy got off cheap with pizza and cola. I squinted for a better look. It was the largest bauble I'd ever seen. Spreading out the photos, I followed the minute-by-minute snippets of the encounter. I flipped toward the end of the pile, watching through the kaleidoscope of photos as a voyeur through the anonymity of the office and my position as Mr. Woodard's assistant. That sounded nice. *Assistant*.

I spied all the way through the couple's four-course dinner and into dessert. This particular café must be their favorite meeting place. I wondered of what significance this restaurant held. Is this where they met through a by-chance encounter? Was it close to their workplace *or* far from anything familiar so as not to get caught? I peeled back the corner of the photos and let them drift back down to the desk like a deck of cards. So many secret meetings caught by the eye of a camera lens, not so secret after all.

I studied the woman's smile and the man's consumption of his lady friend's smoky eyes as they shared the street-side interlude. I could imagine the romantic music playing in the background.

To what lengths and liberties had Mr. Woodard taken to secure his high ratings as a private investigator? I continued through the last few remaining photographs filled with intrigue and apprehension at the direction they were to take. There was a series of photos of laughter, kissing, and the man's gentle caress of the woman's cheek. Page-by-page, watching this real-life drama was like the combination of a horror film and documentary. I half-expected to follow the couple into the throngs of passion and a shared glass of the Crescent City's finest champagne.

The last photos were different. I spread them across Mr. Woodard's desk. The man was paying the dinner check with cash. So, cash was the equivalent of two phones. I shook my head. I wondered if the man had paid for the bauble the same way.

Then Mr. Woodard's photos shifted direction to two men sitting at an adjacent table. Why would Mr. Woodard photograph two men?

The man on the left was wearing sunglasses—at night. Maybe he was a mysterious European celebrity. The second man, in a Hawaiian print short-sleeved shirt and khakis, was passing something across the table toward Mr. Mysterious.

Come on, Mr. Woodard, why did you keep taking pictures?

There had to be something important about *these* photos. So important that Mr. Woodard would call and give me the heebie-jeebies with his secret and detective-like instructions—drill open the filing cabinet and hide the disk.

Mr. Woodard was onto something more than matrimonial indiscretions.

I studied the last series of photos, waiting for the photos to talk to me. The sequence. That might be the key.

Two men arrived at the table during the couple's dinner.

They had cocktails, exchanged dialogue, and then an envelope.

I flipped to the last photograph and dropped with a thud into Mr. Woodard's chair. Mr. Mysterious looked directly into the camera lens.

I wanted to start up Mr. Woodard's car and drive him out of there.

Hurry, I thought, *they see you and your gigantic camera lens!* It was like watching a detective movie in slow motion.

Mr. Mysterious had *made* Mr. Woodard.

Pacing the office, I recited the sequence of events. Mr. Woodard takes cheater photos for a client. Mr. Woodard takes photos of two other men. Why? Was it normal detective curiosity? One man passing an envelope to the other? Highly unlikely that would pique Mr. Woodard's interest. Accidental? I imagined myself as Mr. Woodard held up in the front seat of his car with the camera's long telephoto lens resting on the steering

wheel while he sipped hot black coffee and downed
dinner from the fast food bag left on the dash.

Did Mr. Woodard take the last photos accidentally
or did he have a gut feeling to check out the next table?
Somehow, Mr. Woodard had gotten himself tangled in
a mess. I searched the photo for the missing link. What
was going on? Then I noticed a man at a corner table,
his face shadowed. I looked closer.

It was *him*.

My missing dead man—and he was all wrapped up
in Mr. Woodard's investigation like a take-out meal.

Chapter 19

"Bingo!" I shouted as I snatched the small plastic case from the floor under Mr. Woodard's desk. Mr. Woodard should have done a better job securing its whereabouts. Then a cold chill ran down my spine as last night's escapades swirled through my head. Could *I* have dropped the disk from the folder? No, I was too careful. I pushed away from the thought and its inherent connection to Rudy and set about to the serious business at hand.

Not in my purse. I reminded myself of Mr. Woodard's instructions.

"Don't carry it where it can get pinched," he had said.

Pinched. Where's that? Between my bosoms? In my panties? I winced at the thought of it *down there*. I flipped over the bottom of my skirt and broke the thread of my hem. I pulled several loose loops of hemming free and fed the case through my hem to the side seam of my skirt. I centered my skirt and grabbed the folder.

"I'll find *you*," he had said.

I tried to dismiss images of myself in the bathtub and Mr. Woodard tapping at my door.

I looked up. To my surprise, a woman had been standing in the doorway to Mr. Woodard's office.

"May…may I help you?" I stuttered.

The woman's hair was pulled into a ponytail with short wisps left unattended that shadowed her high cheekbones. Her eyes, like her hair, were the darkest of dark and her lips painted with a dusty rose gloss that glittered against her natural bronzed skin. Despite the heat, she wore ankle-tight soft leather pants with high-heeled sandals. I grew two full dress sizes just looking at her. She pressed into Mr. Woodard's office, leaving me speechless and holding the folder. She circled the office, running her long, thickly polished fingernails along the top of the metal filing cabinets.

"His clientele base seems to be as large as his reputation," she said.

She stopped directly in front of the unlocked cabinet. Her finger hovered over the tab.

"May I help you?" I repeated, trying to usher her from Mr. Woodard's office with an open hand.

"I'm here for my photographs," she said, following me to my desk.

"Your name?" I asked, setting the folder upside down near my computer.

"Dauphine Pascal," she said, extending her reach to shake my hand. My fingers felt like thick sausages against hers. She leaned against the front of my desk. "Mr. Woodard told me to pick up my photographs. Time *is* of the essence."

Her eyes drifted to the folder. I felt protective over my charge and moved the folder with my purse into an empty side drawer. Dauphine Pascal could very well know these people. They were of the same class; high society and country club bred. I felt the need to honor

Mr. Woodard's trust and take control of the folder and the contents therein. I was sure Mr. Woodard could lose his license or be subjected to a lawsuit. I leaned on my elbows, setting a blockade of body and chair in front of the drawer.

Dauphine Pascal swept the wisps of black hair from her eyes with the back of her hand. She was the most attractive woman I had ever seen. Her features and stance were dramatic. Her husband must be out of his mind to cheat on her. *So*, even the beautiful have cheater husbands. I thought of *married* Rudy as he must have ever-so-graciously opened the door for Madame Pascal. I bet he followed her right to the elevator—*if* he was back from his extended hour. The louse. Stood me up for our lunch, opted for an afternoon off with friends, left me sitting at my desk like a fool arranging and rearranging our sandwiches until I found the courage to go downstairs to see why he was late. If I looked like Dauphine Pascal, Rudy would have made it at noon for lunch—or maybe not, since Madame Pascal was apparently the recipient of a cheater's insensitivities as well.

"Mr. Woodard has stepped out, and he didn't leave any instructions on a package to be picked up."

She scanned her phone, swiping the screen with her long fingers.

"There was a message from him earlier today," she said. "Can't seem to find it."

She dropped the phone into a small purse that dangled at her waist and ever so softly, cried. She blotted the dampness from her cheeks. I was amazed. Dauphine

Pascal cried beautifully. No ugly face with snarling lips or snot running from her nose.

"I'm embarrassed. Forgive me, please." She covered her face with a tissue and wept, more like a modest whimper. Not like a wailing banshee, howling between hiccupped gasps for breath.

I wondered if that was something taught in finishing schools: The proper way to cry. How had my mother been so remiss? She had taught me everything else.

Dauphine Pascal's gentle weeping worked. Perhaps had she bawled and carried on, I might have responded differently. People back away from a snot-infested bawling woman. Soft weeps from Dauphine Pascal seemed more like the petals of a prize-winning rose drifting through the air in swirls before resting on the floor.

"I'll make sure he gets your message as soon as possible. Perhaps he can make arrangements to drop the package to you."

She dropped her hands to her lap and sniffled as she spun her wedding ring around her finger. That must be her tick. Some people check the time. Others twitch their lip. Dauphine Pascal spins her ring.

"Your ring is beautiful," I said, pointing to her finger. "Are those sapphires?"

"Blue diamonds," she said, unwavering.

That caught my attention. Couldn't be. Not *my* blue diamonds. I almost laughed. Any other day I would have tossed the paranoid coincidence back to the universe. For the past two days, my world had been consumed with blue diamonds—and in walk blue diamonds.

"Here," she said, sliding the ring from her finger. "Try it on."

"Oh, I couldn't," I said, pressing against the weight of the situation with open hands.

She dropped the ring into my hand. "My husband's an importer-exporter."

The diamond was the largest I had ever seen or held for that matter. Enormous as it was, it's size was accentuated by the circle of smaller blue diamonds tucked in and around the gold setting. I was suddenly aware of my need of a manicure and the thickness of my short fingers. I lowered my head and gave it back. For a brief moment, I was a queen studded in a blue diamond trinket with an eight-pronged setting that overshadowed my knuckles. I released a long sigh.

"Could you please be a dear and check Mr. Woodard's desk for my package? He was very clear with his instructions that I should pick it up tonight after five-thirty." She slid the ring onto her long thin finger.

"I wish I could help you," I said.

She scratched a phone number on a torn piece of paper and handed it to me. "This is my private number. I believe Mr. Woodard already has it."

"I'll make sure to give it to him, personally," I said.

She stopped halfway out the door and turned. "Could you *please* just check Mr. Woodard's desk? It certainly couldn't hurt to check. It would save me a trip. My name should be on the outside of the folder," she said. She clutched the tissue.

My thoughts drifted to my dismal luncheon experience. Dauphine Pascal and I were from different worlds, but the humanness of our sorrow was the same.

I reluctantly nodded. I tried Mr. Woodard's desk drawers. They were locked, just as I had thought. I stepped from Woodard's office to find Dauphine Pascal gone. I ran to my desk. My purse was emptied, the contents strewn about the bottom of the drawer. The folder was missing.

Chapter 20

"Detective Gabby, I'm glad you're still here," I said, as my pulse quickened. I pulled a chair up to his desk. "I know something about the disappearing dead man...and I'd like to report a robbery." I fell into the chair taking a much-needed breath.

Detective Gabby tossed me the morning newspaper. "Business tycoon," he said, tapping at the headlines with a stray paperclip.

"He's not our man," I said, pressing the paper back in his direction.

Detective Gabby dropped his face into his hands and grasped onto his hair. His fingers slowly closed. "What brings you here, Mrs. Crumford?"

"I have a photo of the missing man in my skirt."

A detective to the right of Gabby let out a burst of laughter and ducked behind an open folder.

"Your skirt?" he asked. He leaned into the back of his chair and tossed the paperclip onto his desk.

I scooted to the left of the chair and forced the plastic case through my hem. "The negatives for Mr. Woodard's photos. The missing person is the man in the upper right corner of the last photo. He's sitting at a small table for two, but he's dining alone."

"Negatives?"

"Yes, the unprinted photos on the disk and Dauphine Pascal robbed me of the folder," I said without haste, should some detail escape my memory. "Here's her private number." I handed Gabby the paper. "I need that folder back; I could lose my job. Can't be having the private affairs of people haphazardly in the hands of the wrong people. Why it probably wasn't even her husband. And, what's to say that the people in those photos don't belong to the same country club or horse-riding ring." I stopped for a breath.

"Horse-riding ring?"

"Detective Gabby, it's something the rich do; ride horses and breed blue ribbon colts and children."

"I see," said Detective Gabby.

"I also need my watch. Could you please call over to the lost and found and recover my property? It's a small-faced watch with a narrow band. I believe I left it on the table."

"Mrs. Crumford...."

"I interviewed our doorman, Rudy, on your behalf."

"Your doorman?"

"And I must say, I was a little disappointed in the fact that you gentlemen were remiss in your policing duties," I whispered, wagging a loose finger at the other detectives.

"So, I interviewed Garvey."

"Garvey?"

If Detective Gabby had on eyeglasses, he would have been glaring at me over the top rim like Mr. Woodard.

"He saw the dead man on the elevator," I said, firmly.

"Was he flat on the floor or propped up in the corner?"

"He died in my office."

"Was incoherent," said Detective Gabby.

"Dead. No doubt about it," I stated. "I've held a dying person in my arms; I know what it feels like." I broke out in tears, shocking myself with the sudden outburst. "I held Eddie in my arms as he took his final breath."

Detective Gabby rose from his chair and motioned for one of the other officers to bring me a glass of water. Why *do* men run for water when a woman is in distress? An officer brought the glass, and I guess the personal attention was soothing. Detective Gabby let me sit for a while.

"How long have you been alone, Mrs. Crumford?"

"Five years."

"I'm sorry for your loss," said Detective Gabby.

"I am, too," I said.

"How old are you?" he asked.

"Sixty-two."

"Wouldn't you rather stay home and bake cookies or something? Watch your favorite television programs and home shopping networks?" asked the detective.

I slumped over my lap. I cradled my forehead in my hand as the throbbing intensified behind my eyes. It was a mistake to come in here. It was a mistake ever to think that I could be taken seriously or have something to offer other than a clean house and a hot meal.

"Well, Detective Gabby, I have no one to bake cookies for, and I do not own a television. I don't drive. I have a home stacked so full of memories I can't breathe. I don't want to be home. I've been there for five years without

Eddie. The walls are not changing. They are the same walls day and night. They say nothing. They offer nothing. They provide nothing except a place to sleep. I was not the one who died."

An officer set a box of tissue in front of me. I tried to remember the proper way to cry as I patted the tears from my cheek.

"I still have something to offer the world," I whispered. "You can have a good laugh as soon as I leave." I stood and squared the chair in front of the desk.

"I'm sorry, that was not my intention. Perhaps this case seems like more than it is because you are looking for an emotional diversion, similar to what you might find from watching television or the shopping network. That was all I meant."

"Maybe I should be the one to judge what I need. Thank you for your time, Detective Hugo Gabby. If you don't mind, I would like to relieve myself of my duties with this case."

"Don't worry; I can see myself out."

Police work wasn't for me. For forty-one years I've waited for an opportunity to spread my wings, and I guess it is not with the police department. I was exhausted. Worn out. Physically drained. I hadn't managed to unravel the mysteries of the past two days, but I had unraveled myself. I thought of myself sitting in the chair opposite Detective Gabby. Disemboweled on the police station floor. I was surprised he hadn't called for a mop.

I wandered down Royal toward the bus stop, keenly aware of everything. The birds. The smells. The sounds.

Traffic was bumper to bumper. People were shouting and rushing. Rushing to where? To their tomorrows? Their tomorrows will be spent on tomorrows until there aren't any more tomorrows left. Then they'll focus on the yesterdays. How about if everyone lived in the space of the present moment. I stopped mid-step and looked around. Not one person was taking the time to acknowledge with whom they just bumped shoulders. Not one person was aware of the chirping of birds or the hanging baskets of color and bloom that adorned the upper balcony of the corner building. I wanted to shout. *You're all keepers of time. There's no guarantee for your length of stay. Stop and harvest life's blessings.* But who would listen?

I passed an older woman dragging a cart full of groceries and a bundle of flowers. Flowers. I wondered if she would take the time to smell those flowers or were the flowers expected to merely occupy the space of lost moments. Their blossoms to wilt before their sweet fragrance enjoyed. How sad for the state of life in this world as we know it. Busy sprinting through every moment packed full with nothingness.

I stood on the corner and waited for the bus. Lost in myself. Lost in memories of Eddie. Lost in my age and time ill spent. My face once painted with life's fragrances, was now patinaed with furrows and sunspots. I've been put on a shelf and dismissed until my last blossom drops, and the world can toss aside my stem. That's what I felt like today.

I felt my age.

Thank you, Detective Gabby for gifting me the awareness of myself.

I turned to the storefront window and looked at myself standing in my nakedness before my own eyes. I took in a deep breath. So, this was life. It was what you made of it, and it was what you saw in it. I liked my flowery skirts and outdated ideals. I like my flower-topped shoes and pocketbooks of different colors. I inhaled a long deep breath of the shared polluted air, full of car emissions and spent breath. We were all in this together. Couldn't they see? We shared the same earth, same air. Terrible to discard the aged. Terrible to disregard each other. Terrible indeed.

I hopped onto my bus and took a seat. Before the bus driver could close the door, a hand forced it open again.

Not again!

It was him.

The bus-fare bully.

Chapter 21

I held onto the seatback in front of me. My gut screamed to g*et off the bus!* But my head responded with another round of bolting throbs. What are the odds of seeing Mickey Mullen again?

Mickey dropped the quarters into the fair box. *My quarters.* It was the perfect ending to a perfectly horrible day—my money used as the tally to put Mouse on the bus with me. Mickey smacked a tightly twisted envelope across the palm of his hand as he sauntered down the aisle.

I rested my aching head against the cool window-pane and closed my eyes. The envelope lingered in my mind. Like the exchanged envelope at the restaurant. Now tightly twisted. Pointed. Sharp. Easily tossed aside or recycled.

A weapon!

Ingenious, I thought. Poke me in the eye with the envelope and run off with my handbag. I hugged my purse and pinched my eyes closed even tighter. This would have been a good day to start wearing my glasses.

I was too tired to get off the bus and wait for another.

Too hungry to delay dinner at home.

I just wanted to sit alone on the bus for a peaceful ride home. I didn't want a confrontation with a bully. I didn't want my eyes poked out with a sharp envelope, and I didn't want to lose my handbag—even if it was practically empty.

My head and heart still throbbed from the luncheon disaster. I'd been abandoned and humiliated. I just wanted to climb into bed with a half-gallon of ice cream. I just wanted to sit alone on the bus for a peaceful ride home.

Detective Gabby's disparaging comments cycled and swirled through my head. He had no right to treat me like that. Not Gabby. Not Rudy. Not Mickey the Mouse. Not Eddie.

I turned in the seat and faced the bully with both eyes open.

"If you think you're going to poke my eyes out and steal my purse, you better think twice. I know karate." The words spewed from my mouth.

He leaned over the back of my seat. "Poke your eyes out?"

"Sit somewhere else," I said through clenched teeth. "I saw your picture. At the *police* station," I whispered. "Mickey Mullen. Aka the Mouse? Purse thief. Eye stabber."

His mouth puckered. He jumped to his feet, tearing his way to the front of the bus. "Let me off!" he shouted.

"I can't just stop in the middle of the road," the bus driver shouted back.

"Now!" yelled Mickey, pulling a knife from his pocket. He pointed it at the driver.

Someone in the front seat screamed.

Passengers crouched down in their seats.

The bus driver stopped mid lane.

Mickey, the Mouse Mullen, jumped from the top step and ran.

I was speechless as I watched Mikey Mullen and the peace sign disappear around a corner.

The driver called the dispatcher.

Several passengers left the area immediately.

I waited to give a statement to the police.

"It was Mickey Mullen, the Mouse," I calmly stated to the uniformed officer writing the report. "He was going to stab the bus driver with a knife."

"How do you know this man?" asked the officer.

"He was following me," I said. "Detective Gabby gave me his name."

"Detective Gabby?" he asked, scrawling on a small notepad. He looked up from the pad as though he was seeing me for the first time.

"I don't drive, which is why I take public transportation."

There was a pause.

"Have a seat on the bench," he instructed.

I went over the details in my head. I had told it as it had happened. I wanted to go home. Reluctantly, I sat, waited, and watched as the remaining passengers dispersed through the crowded street. The bus driver shut the doors, a few familiar ticks of the flashing turn signal and I was alone on the bench. I exhaled. Even the bus driver had been allowed to leave. Why was this taking so long? I wanted to be sitting in my garden sipping tea with my feet nestled in the cool grass.

"Mrs. Crumford, you seem to be the eye of a hurricane this week," said Detective Gabby.

I was happy to hear his voice.

"You wouldn't believe me if I told you."

"Mouse?" asked Detective Gabby.

"With a knife."

"I'm going to have an officer drive you home where you can have a fresh cup of tea with cream and sugar."

Chapter 22

I centered myself on the sofa, trying to catch the hint of a cross-breeze from the opened windows as I sipped on my iced tea. The lace curtains barely danced across the wooden sill. Condensation ran down the side of the glass and dripped onto my lap. I was too tired to wipe away the water droplets and too hot to care. It was too late and too hot to eat. The house was stifling, just like the day had been. I craned my neck, relieving the tightness that ran from my shoulders and down into my lower back.

Mr. Woodard's note sat precariously on the sofa next to me.

Give the disk to Gabby, -W Woodard.

The disk was already in the hands of Detective Gabby. Woodard could deal with him. My private investigating days were over! The past two days had been like living a real-life mystery dinner theater, except I hadn't had dinner. Was Mr. Woodard hanging around my house, waiting for my return home? Or, had he nonchalantly walked up, crammed the note in behind the screen door, and continued without one missed step of his elongated stride. Creepiness crawled up and down my spine. It felt as though he was still out there, lurking around my door, waiting for me to hand off the disk. I was sorry I had missed him. There were questions I needed answered.

My thoughts drifted around the disk, Detective Gabby, Mickey Mullen, and then to the woman with white eyes. I straightened the coffee-tabled photo of Eddie, wishing he were here. So much had happened.

I ran my fingertip over the outline of his face. We were at my parent's farm that day. I closed my eyes and almost smelled the farm-fresh air. We had just gotten married. Eddie was strong and bigger than life. I sought protection in his arms, wishing for a happy life and a family. A peaceful existence free from compartments and the scrutiny of my mother's eye. I had convinced myself that married life with Eddie would be a dream-come-true of unending possibilities.

Eddie used to tell me that he wore my heart in his breast pocket. I guess that was his cumbersome way of saying that he loved me. My Eddie, or Edward as he preferred to hear from me. Eddie was the familiar name reserved for his friends and family. I often wondered what he thought we were. After all, we *were* married. So, Edward was spoken from my lips, and Eddie was savored for my affectionate thoughts in the privacy of my mind. Eddie had just landed an accounting job at a large firm in New Orleans. In planning for our future, he had purchased a two-sided shotgun-style house. He knew that owning both sides would provide a constant influx of income once we were able to reduce the mortgage. Originally, we were planning to move into something larger after children came along. Children never came. We never moved. Eddie settled into his job. I settled into mundane.

I set up housekeeping partnered with two traveling companions; my vivid imagination coupled with myself. Silently, I feared I had a split-personality. Maybe I was meant to be partnered with a twin, and the other twin didn't make it to the conception on time. So, there I was left alone traveling down the birth canal toward the waiting arms of my mother and the proper compartments of my segmented life. I do have conversations with myself. I laugh aloud when I see the humor in a situation. I know what's going on when I dig down deep. Hours spent alone constitute a form of meditation and reflection. I know my chronic babbling is merely the ceremonial scarring from emotional deprivation. I've grown so used to me that it would seem awkward if I didn't express myself in verbose orations from time to time. In fact, half the time I don't know who's talking. Me or the other me. I ask myself, *did I say that aloud or was it my imagination*? Unsettling to others, I'm sure, watching an old woman walking and talking to herself.

I sat back on the sofa and laughed, revisiting one of my strolls on one of my Green Line walking excursions. It was a heavenly spot. Birds and butterflies, dappled in sunlight, were playful in motion across a freshly watered lawn. Then the pleasantries of the afternoon came to a screaming halt. Their mocking laughter grew louder as they crept in behind me. Teenagers about fourteen-years-of-age, bold and arrogant in their cause. Chests puffed like roosters but cackling more like hens. I turned on my heels and scrunched my mouth. I spoke louder to the birds, telling them not to worry, that these coyotes were harmless. The surprise on their faces was worth the blisters from following *them* for three blocks babbling and clucking about their pants below their hips and hair covering their eyes.

Eddie and I were unable to have children and adoption had never come up in our conversations. I was unsure if it was because Eddie was afraid to hurt my feelings or if his feelings were hurt. We wanted children. Several years into our marriage, when my mother pressed the subject of proper timing to start a family, Eddie responded that having me around *was* like having a child. It was an endearing statement at first. But in retrospect, it was nothing more than a hurtful response to a hurtful situation. Why was it that men seemed to need to chop at the knees? Wasn't it bad enough I couldn't have children? Wasn't it bad enough I was a stay-at-home wife with a stay-at-home life? That washed walls and polished floors were my only claim to fame?

I had thought my headstone should read, *Here lies Harriet Crumford. She kept a very clean house.*

I strived for a proper amount of happiness by wringing out a life that consisted of short scampers to the grocery store, superficial hellos, and the marital passion Eddie regulated as much as our checking account.

Wrestling with thoughts of marital passion, I rested my head on the arm of the sofa. I had never seen my husband naked. I had felt his manhood press against and in my body, but I had never seen him naked. I wondered if that was how it was in other marriages.

Why? I clenched my fists and cried. Why did he deprive me of life? Why did he deprive me of the joys of being a young wife? He had a life full of acquaintances, friends, and fellow office workers. Did he not think once about the jail he prepared for me? Didn't he consider how long and arduous the days were for me? Days and nights by myself.

Emptiness filled me to the core. He was probably standing over me with my mother at his side. I covered my face with the palms of my hands and wept.

What is happiness? Bills paid? A large house? My life was routine, but not happy or fulfilling. I had to invent a life with a social calendar and companionship. Maybe living with me *was* like living with a child, but it was how I survived. I cleaned, and I cooked. I arranged and rearranged the furniture only to put everything back in its original place. Eddie dealt with numbers all day. Eddie demanded order. The table where the table belonged was the equivalent of two plus two equaling four. My totals always added to three or five. I had wanted happiness. The comfort of loving and being loved. Beyond a house, career, fancy clothes, or high-society friends.

Happiness harnessed in the form of human connections.

Eddie deprived me of happiness! He deprived me of love and companionship. Oh, he came home every night, but in an empty shell. Then, he died. Everything in my life came to a screaming halt. The little companionship he offered was gone. My financial security ended. Life became a merry-go-round of ups and downs. Damn! He left me old and forgotten like junk mail and empty water bottles discarded and caught between the weeds along the sidewalk.

I sobbed, wiping my cheeks with the back of my hand. "By the way, Eddie, if you can hear me—I hope you've noticed—I've rearranged a few things in the house!"

I mixed pots and pans with the cups and saucers. Two plus two making three. It felt like the day I tossed that girdle into the garbage.

Freeing.

Eddie had left for work and left me behind *and* in place like the furniture. Just like the furniture! Every day the dinner arranged on the table along with me. Never did I consider making other preparations or simply not going home.

"I loved you, Eddie," I whispered to the photograph. "You never thought you would die first. You *counted* on that. Well, for the first time in your life, you counted wrong!" I swiveled my feet to the floor. The floor felt cool and soothing.

I pulled a dusty bottle of Merlot from the back of the linen closet. Who says you have to keep linens in a linen closet? It was free space and in my world free space means just that. I hugged the bottle close to my breast.

Here's to free space and lost chances.

Here's to cups under the sink and hairspray on the dresser instead of the vanity and to answering the phone in Mr. Woodard's office.

Here's to the poor soul that died in my arms yesterday.

And here's to an end of a head-throbbing day.

I poured myself a healthy tumbler of red wine, allowing my body to sway with the gentle jingle of the wind chimes in the window and gulped down half the glass before catching a breath. I savored the sting it left in my mouth. A drop of spilled wine settled on the counter. Like me.

I had settled on a marriage built on the paper slabbing of a marriage license instead of a loving and solid foundation.

Here's to my marriage!

Downing another gulp of wine, I reflected on my stupidity. My dumbness about life. I wondered if Eddie had a good laugh about that with *her*? I crumpled to the counter and fell into my hands, sobbing.

Wiping my face with the dishcloth, I toasted to my failed marriage and to my failed life. I toasted to my failed attempt to filter into society and my failed attempt to make a difference on the planet. Three-quarters of the bottle later, the wine, like my marriage, had left a sour taste in my mouth.

Sauntering into the living room, I turned on the radio. The scratch marks were still on the floor from where the old Victrola has once stood. I rubbed the marks with my bare foot. The spot that marked secret letters scented and neatly tied with satin and silk ribbons. Heartfelt love letters from her to him. How could I have been so stupid? I wonder if she saw him naked. Had he made love to her with the lights on?

I gulped the rest of the wine and wiped my mouth with the back of my hand.

All the business trips and late hours at the office. He held me prisoner in this house with my imagination while he carried on with two lives!

To think that all those years *my* marriage built on faith and trust and Eddie's was built on a slab of scented letters.

Circling my finger over the armrest of the sofa, I relived the tormented weeks and months spent in tears, slowly unwrapping my marriage through those envelopes.

She had beautiful penmanship. Long and elegant. Not short and thick. More than likely she was heavenly designed like her fine-tipped calligraphy pen while I was molded from a thick permanent marker.

I couldn't allow myself to revisit the funeral, scanning the attendees from my mind's eye. Where was she? Was she married as well? Was she there with her husband? I might have liked to know who she was and why she stole my life. I pondered the encounter. Demanding her attention. Demanding answers. I imagined her face blush as I announced that Eddie was dead and her *services* were no longer needed.

I could only hope that Eddie was floating overhead, bearing witness to the pain and sheer misery of his scandalous behavior. The worst part was when I finally found the courage to read those letters. She addressed each one to *Eddie*. The intimate details were not nearly as devastating as the fact that *she* called him Eddie!"

Heat surged through my body as I relived the violation and betrayal. I closed my eyes and prayed for relief. My breath heaved from the weighted memories of searching the house for hidden remnants of his time spent in her company. Tokens tucked away to ease his continued masquerade with me. I thought of necklaces bought and paid for with cash. Two phones. Two lives. So many questions forever left unanswered.

I became a lunatic on a mission to eradicate and destroy, unable to live in a house with *her*. I found the stash by accident while rearranging the furniture. Hidden in the Victrola, right under my nose for all those years. Shockingly, I only needed a hammer. Probably could have sold the bloody thing, but the money would have been soiled and vile. Every little scrap and component of that Victrola made its way to the trash along with the letters, a locket, and a scarf.

I opened another bottle of wine and poured another glass.

Stumbling into the bathroom, I vomited. My head pounded. I stretched my legs out on the cool bathroom tile floor and rested against the wall. I wished I had a dollar for every time I had scrubbed the bathroom while I was as naked as a baby's bottom naked! I laughed at the consideration the people in my life would have taken at that. How improper for *Harriet* to clean her bathroom while naked.

I reached to flush, but the bathroom walls swayed. Let the vomit sit in the toilet overnight. Who cares? Who's going to know? Is Detective *Hugo Gabby* coming to my house tonight to give me a ticket for an unflushed toilet?

Pulling myself up from the floor, I fixed my hair and washed my hands. Begrudgingly, I flushed the toilet and leaned in toward the mirror.

"That's not all I did, Mother!" I shouted in sheer delight of my drunkenness. "I also danced around the house naked!"

Stripping down past my skivvies, I danced naked from one end of the house to the other, free as a butterfly.

Chapter 23

Everything has a time and a place.

Right now, my place was behind my desk, Charlie's place was on a different street, and Rudy's was still being out-to-lunch.

"Rudy?" I asked as Garvey held the door open for the stream of office workers racing the clock.

"Didn't show up this morning."

That was unusual. From the evil shadows of my hurt ego, I secretly hoped he was home, hovered over the toilet with an internal upset resulting from his lunch with *friends*. Internal twists and turns from the wrenching discomfort of bad food and too much drink.

The ache between my eyes reminded me of last night's wine. I teetered between self-pity and my feelings for Rudy. We would have to talk.

Car exhaust and rumbling engines were like an early morning's alarm clock. The kind you can't shut off regardless of the buttons pushed, and knobs turned. I shuffled toward the door, wishing for a day minus noise and chaos. Today, I savored the quiet and mundane.

I rode the elevator pinched between shoulders and briefcases with a packed lunch, and the office mail tucked under my arm. I removed my pumps and silently walked to my office; no need for extra attention this morning. I welcomed the thought of peace and quiet.

The office door was ajar. I was sure I had closed and locked it last night. I cracked the door and poked my head in for a quick look. My desk was untouched. Everything was as I had left it. Maybe Garvey had stopped in for the pliers, or maybe Mr. Woodard had a change of plans. I inched the door open. I swallowed hard around the lump in my throat. It wasn't my fault the folder was stolen, *and* if Mr. Woodard had maintained regular working hours he could have claimed the events of the past three days instead of me!

I eased the door closed. Silly me, getting all paranoid for nothing. I *tisk-tisked* my way around my desk and flipped on my computer. My thoughts lingered over Dauphine Pascal and plausible explanations. If I had a locking desk like Mr. Woodard, the folder would have remained safe and secure. Maybe it was time for a new desk or a set of filing cabinets that I could lock at will. I tucked my lunch in the corner of the desk and readied myself to check messages.

There were two messages from clients wishing to settle their tab discreetly. The third message was a flux of expletives sandwiched between tears from Lilly. I gathered the messages and the mail and knocked on Mr. Woodard's door.

There was no answer.

I knocked again and waited a few seconds before opening the door.

The mail slid from my hand.

Mickey Mullen was sitting at Mr. Woodard's desk.

Mickey smiled, exposing his thick front teeth. He had on the same tee shirt, and his hair was uncombed. He leaned back in the chair and put his feet up on the corner of Mr. Woodard's desk. He toyed with an open knife, swiping it back and forth across the knees of his soiled jeans.

I retreated a few steps and reached aimlessly for the door. Someone rushed me from behind. A hand clamped around my arm. Something sharp poked my ribs.

"I don't have any money," I said, trying to pry free.

"We have an appointment," said Mickey with an edge to his voice.

"Oh," I said, nodding my head. "If you don't mind, I have things to do before Mr. Woodard gets here. Make yourselves comfortable."

"Our appointment is with you, Mrs. Crumford." Mickey dropped his feet to the floor.

I tried to shift away from the man. He jabbed deeper into my ribs and tightened his grip. I couldn't move.

"Let's take a walk," said Mickey.

"Please, no."

"Let's not make this uncomfortable," said Mickey, rounding the desk. The other man pulled me closer to his body. He smelled of cigarettes and coffee.

"Where are we going?" I asked, extending my arm toward the floor to retrieve the mail.

Mickey kicked the envelopes across the floor.

"Leave it!" the man shouted.

"I have to get home. I have a sick husband," I said, sputtering and stammering for words.

The man twisted my arm from behind. I fell forward and caught a glimpse of my assailant. My heart hit the floor. I had seen him before. He was the man with the metal hand. Rudy was right; this man was not a war hero.

Mickey swiped my purse from the desk. "Your husband is dead," he said. "You can stop with the games."

They tucked in alongside me, pushing me down the hall toward the elevator. I pleaded with God for an elevator full of people. Maybe someone would come to my rescue. We waited for the elevator door to open. I pulled to the left only to feel the cold metal hand pressed further into my ribs.

Where were the nosy receptionists now?

"You try to pull anything, I'll cut your throat," said Mickey, brandishing the knife in front of my face.

I stood rigidly fixed to life, pushing down the panic and cleared my head. I *could* try to force myself to pass out from hyperventilation. They couldn't stab me in an elevator full of people. Someone would have to call a doctor. Maybe the doctor down the hall would come. I could whisper in his ear as the dying man did to me, except I would be telling him to save me from the guy with the metal hand. I wanted to scream. Maybe those were going to be *my* last words. *Man with the metal hand.* I could see Detective Gabby scratching his head, sorrowful for not listening to me.

I don't want those for my last words.

I don't want last words.

"Please, don't kill me."

The elevator doors opened. The tip of Mickey's knife pressed into the small of my back. I tried to make eye contact with someone—anyone, but no one noticed me. Garvey was still at the door.

"Leaving already, Miss Hattie?" he asked.

Get help! I screamed from inside my head. Rudy would have known something was wrong. The man with the metal hand nudged me toward the curb. A long black limo pulled curbside, and I was roughly encouraged to get into the back seat. Mickey Mullen sat across from me with the open knife. The other man sat practically on top of me. He tapped the door lock with his metal hand. Mickey knocked on the tinted window behind the driver's head.

I stared at Mickey. "You *were* following me."

His eyes furrowed.

"I gave you quarters," I said.

He leaned forward and smacked my handbag free from my lap. Rolling quarters, dog biscuits, and the remainder of contents from my purse scattered across the carpeted floor. "This ain't about no quarters," said Mickey.

"What do you want from me?" I asked.

"Look at what this old bat carries in her purse," taunted Mickey, ignoring my question.

"You working a case with Gabby?" interrupted the man with the hooked hand.

"Detective Gabby? Working with me?"

"She's lying," shouted Mickey.

"Boring, boring, boring is my life," I said.

"It didn't look too boring last night." Mickey chuckled.

I brought my hand to my mouth. "I'm feeling sick." I cradled myself and leaned over my lap. "I need to get out. I'm going to throw up," I said, reaching for the car door. The other man grabbed me by the back of my neck and squeezed. I thought he would crack my spine if I didn't oblige.

"Too much wine and dancing last night?" asked Mickey.

Mickey was at my house! The thought settled heavy in my gut.

He saw me.

Dance.

Naked.

Mickey snorted in private laughter. The man next to me picked up one of my loose quarters from the limo floor and tossed it at Mickey hitting him square in the forehead.

"Hey, what do you think you're doing?" shouted Mickey.

"You're a sick fuck," said the man with the hooked hand.

"Since when did you become a priest, Vic?" asked Mickey, rubbing his forehead.

The man had a name. This was not good. They never let the hostages hear their names. Then reality hit me between the eyes. I could not breathe. My heart was in my throat. *They're not going to let me go.* My mind raced. I had to get away. *Breathe deeply.* Wait for the right moment. I had to stay alert. My life depended on it.

I pressed into the back of the seat and waited for the opportunity to lunge for the door.

I had been violated in so many different directions.

I could hear my mother's words; everything has a time and a place.

Wait for the right time.

I had to take a chance. Better to end up under the tires of a truck than wherever it was these two were taking me. I threw myself across the seat, then grabbed for the door with both hands. Mickey backhanded me across the side of my face. Vic pulled me from the door by the back of my neck and slammed my face down onto the leather-upholstered seat.

"You should have minded," snorted Vic.

I thought he would pinch off my head. My lungs burned for air. His grip tightened. The limo seat smelled like Mr. Woodard's red leather chair, reminding me of days bordering on the mundane. Why hadn't I gone for help when I found the office door ajar? I knew the answer.

My life had been directed by a *what would people think* attitude instead of just following my gut. So what if I wore old shoes! So what! So what if I had mistakenly run for help again or just not gone to work in the first place. Why didn't I stay home today? Why didn't I live out the remainder of my days in the proper cupboard, properly shelved next to the cups and saucers? I wished to put it all back the way it was, the Victrola, the furniture, the boring days spent looking out through the lace curtain for dreams.

I bartered with God and every saint I could remember to get me out of this mess, promising not to give a hankering about appearances and the thoughts of others. Promising to follow my gut and, most of all, promising to acknowledge my blessings whether they're my expanding waistline or graying hair. I promised to be happy with who I am and where I am and forget about tomorrows. I promised never to take safety for granted. I promised never to wish for a leather-upholstered chair. I cleared my throat and gasped for air from the corner of my mouth.

I struggled for breath through my flattened nose; fear raged through my gut. My neck burned from Vic's grip. I felt the dampness of fresh tears between my cheek and the seat. I cried for fear that this might be the end of my life. I rocked to the motion of turns and stops. I counted the right and left turns as a mental diversion. I recognized the familiar hum of the streetcar traveling the tracks and the chimes from a church. Streetcar and church. I made a mental map of the turns and sounds. Where were they were taking me? A saxophonist began a fresh tune. We were leaving the French Quarter. I felt the loud bass thud from a car sharing the adjacent lane. We must be at a traffic light. I heard the street musicians strumming and blowing their tunes in the background, and then silence. I heard the whishing of fast-moving vehicles overhead. We must have crossed under an overpass. We were heading north, or east—maybe west. Maybe in circles. Then quiet. Time pulled and twisted like summer taffy.

Vic tapped the window with his hook.

I pressed my face into the leather and held my breath, preferring death by self-suffocation.

The limo stopped.

Mickey was the first out.

Vic grabbed a handful of my hair and pulled.

I yelled as I squeezed his wrist, forcing my nails into the fleshly part of the palm of his hand. He wedged the crook of his hook under my chin. I released my hold and inched across the seat of the limo leaving my purse and the contents scattered across the floor of the limo.

I didn't care. The bus pass held no value. I did not want to get out of the limo. I wanted to slam the door shut and yell for the driver to go as fast as possible away from the past three days.

Vic finished yanking me out by the arm. Mickey slammed the door shut and knocked twice on the roof of the vehicle. The limo disappeared down a side street, leaving me to wonder if the driver would call the police.

They marched me half a block before turning down a side street. Mickey had an open knife stuck in my rib. Tears ran down my cheek as I quietly cried for the loss of hope. There were no passersby, no children playing on the street. There were no shop clerks. No shops. It was a ghost town; the lasting impact of Katrina stamped upon this impoverished part of the city. There was nowhere to run and no one to hear. I felt a vague familiarity with this area of the city. Vic grabbed my elbow and pushed me along the street. I tripped over the uneven cement. They pulled me to my feet.

"Try that again, and you'll eat pavement," said Vic, under his breath.

I forced myself to memorize details. Splotches of discarded chewing gum hardened on the sidewalk. A garbage-strewn street along an empty lot. An empty shopping cart under the overpass. Flattened cardboard, empty bottles, and a single sneaker. Time had halted to a snapshot view with each blink. Loud music poured from a multilevel building, blocks away. A tattered curtain limply hung out of a broken window. A baby cried in the distance. A tomcat meowed from an overhead landing, and I nearly fainted. The buildings were old, and the plaster walls long ago cracked. They're taking a chance, I thought, letting me see where I'm going. A dog barked from across the street. I squinted trying to read the street sign. Damn glasses were at home.

Two blocks down, I could see where the road forked at a small corner bar. I had been through here before in a funeral parade. The slow and mournful dirge had become an up-tempo celebration of life with a brass band worthy of a standing ovation. The music and dancing were intoxicating. People from the sidewalk's edge joined in and dropped out of the parade along the way. I ran to join in, captivated by the deliriously happy music and dancing. It felt like my soul had been set free. I had lost track of the twists and turns, and the blocks traveled. The parade ended at a backyard barbecue far from my comfort zone. Suddenly, I was aware of the complexities of social differences and was clueless as to where I was or how to get home. A gentle man of soft ebony color had offered food, but I declined. It was his wife's funeral parade. His hands thick with calluses, his back bent with age. He had me escorted by his grandchildren to the bus stop. They waited less than patiently. I was sorrowful for their loss for they were indeed a lovely family and I wished they had been my neighbors.

The neighborhood was now barely recognizable; the houses abandoned and boarded up. Shameful for the money allotted to this part of the city for repairs after the rising waters. Mickey and Vic forced me down an alley between a row of buildings with shared common walls. It smelled of urine. They dragged me across a street and through another alley adjacent to a warehouse where a homeless man sat on the edge of the sidewalk, his back against a broken light pole.

I stopped straight in my tracks.

"Make a sound, and I'll cut you right here," whispered Mickey, as they skirted me around the man.

It was Charlie.

One in a million chance that in this part of the city, on these empty streets, the only one to see me was *Charlie*. I looked over my shoulder, trying to send him a mental message to call for help. Why was he so far from his regular corner?

"Hattie," mouthed Charlie, but no sound came out. He started to his feet.

"Stop!" Charlie shouted, pulling a handgun from his pocket.

Mickey crouched behind me for cover.

I tried to wrap my mind around Charlie with a gun. My Charlie was going to save me. He'd force them to let me go.

Then, from the corner of my eye, I saw the flash as the bullet exploded from the barrel of Vic's gun.

I lost my balance as Charlie hit the ground. His gun dropped to the ground. Blood rushed from his wrist.

Charlie.

Shot.

"Keep going," shouted Mickey, yanking me back onto my feet. He shoved me around the corner of a building.

I heard another shot.

"Let's get out of here!" shouted Vic, his breath hurried.

They pulled me towards a set of stairs in a back alleyway, into a building, and onto a connecting catwalk into another building. I tried to memorize the twisted path. I *had* to memorize the path. I had to know how to get back to Charlie. My Charlie. Shot twice. Probably dead.

Dead because of me. I might as well have shot him myself.

I stumbled across a rusty metal fire escape to an open window. Vic crawled through first. Mickey pushed me from behind. I fell forward onto the filthy floor.

"You're going to kill me, aren't you?" I asked.

"Keep going," said Mickey, shoving me in the shoulder toward a warped wooden door. Vic kicked the door open. It was a large room with garbage and tattered blankets heaped in the corner. In the center of the room was a thick sheet of plastic. In the middle of the plastic sat a metal chair. Empty room and a chair on plastic. I gasped for air.

"I'm just an old woman," I pleaded. "I'm of no use to you."

"You're gonna give me a little dance. *Like last night.* She's a good dancer, Vic," said Mickey. He ran his tongue over his teeth.

"You sick little man," I muttered. "You are nothing more than a *mouse!*" The words flew from my mouth like shots from a cannon. Splashed hues of my brain and life flew before my eyes in a grand array of color against the cracked and peeling plaster walls. In one swift motion, Mickey yanked me off my feet. I landed with a thud on my hip.

"What are you doing?" shouted Vic. He leaned over and grabbed me by the arm. I tried to pull from his grasp.

"Listen, Vic," shouted Mickey, "you can't tell me what to do!"

Vic smacked Mickey against the wall. Mickey rose to his feet with a fisted hand.

Vic leaned into him and smiled.

"Go ahead. Take your best shot."

I scanned the hall for an exit. Better to take my chances than end up in the Mississippi. It was now or never.

Vic slammed me against the wall. My ankle twisted, I fell back to the floor. I took hold of my pump and walloped the metal-handed man along the side of his chin with my shoe. I dragged the jagged edge of the worn heel through the flesh of his cheek. A thick and uneven white line of raw flesh quickly filled with blood. Vic fell backward and drew his hand to the side of his face. Mickey stood with his hand still clenched, his eyes wide, mouth open.

I took off as fast as my short legs would take me.

I ran along the hall, down the catwalk, and onto the street. I kicked off the other shoe and turned down an unfamiliar street. Where was Charlie? Where was I? I crossed corners and ran through alleys. My lungs craved air. I had to keep going. I had to get away. I had to get help. I stumbled over sidewalk trash and picked myself up. There was life ahead. Horns honked. People were on the street. Life. I ran into a small corner store past a man behind the counter. I pressed through the narrow aisles of canned goods and laundry soaps toward the back door.

"Hey, you can't go back there!" shouted the store clerk.

I ran out the back door and across to another street corner hurdling broken glass and trash.

I kept running, all the way onto a stopped bus just as the doors were about to shut.

"Step on it!" I cried, motioning for the driver to close the doors. "I'm being chased." I grabbed onto the handrail. I thought I would collapse.

I was shoeless, moneyless, gasping for air.

The driver scratched his jaw.

"Please," I said between breaths, "is there anyone who could spare the fare? I would be glad to reimburse you." Tears ran down my face.

"Let me in," shouted Mickey, banging on the bus door. "She's my mother. She's confused. I've been chasing after her all morning. Look how she's dressed. She's crazy. She's shoeless. Let me on the bus!" He pounded on the door with both fists.

"I'm not crazy. Please, you've got to believe me," I pleaded, still gasping for breath. I gently touched the driver's arm. "My life depends on it." I squeezed the handrail. "I lost my shoes because *he* was chasing me."

"Open up!" shouted Mickey, pounding on the door.

The bus driver hesitated with his hand over the door lever. How *could* he believe me? I was the one without shoes. My blouse hung loosely around my waist. My stockings, torn. My hair, messed. I was sure what little makeup I had was now running down my face.

"I'm not crazy!" I trembled. "Call Detective Hugo Gabby; he can explain everything." I scanned the faces of the passengers, praying someone would believe me.

"I'll cover her fare!" shouted a woman from the back of the bus. Her voice was husky and full.

"Come on," pleaded Mickey still pounding on the door.

"I'll take responsibility!" shouted the woman. She pressed forward with an outreached hand and dropped the money into the fare box. "Go!"

"Thank you," I said, just above a whisper.

"Bastard," she said, watching Mickey shake his fist at the moving bus. "Sit with me."

My cheeks burned as I passed down the aisle of the moving bus, barefoot—and humbled by the comfort this stranger had offered.

"Mind your business," she said to an old man staring at me through narrowed eyes.

"Do you have a phone?" I whispered, hoping not to draw more unwanted attention in my direction. "My friend was shot back there."

"Landline. No cell," she said.

"Can someone call the police?" I asked, a little louder. I scanned the passengers, trying to make eye contact with someone—*anyone.*

I waited. Some frowned and looked away.

"My friend was shot back there," I added. "Someone, please, call and report a shooting."

Still no response.

"The police are probably already there," said a lanky teen. I pleaded to his heart through tear-filled eyes. He nodded and dialed 9-1-1.

"The police will find your friend," said the woman, motioning me to an empty seat. "Have a place to go for the night?" I shook my head no. "Come home with me." I scooted in against the window. She sat down next to me. She was small in stature, but this tiny woman had the courage of a giant and the wisdom of an old soul. This woman had saved my life. I wished to thank her. I wished to hug her and kiss her and unload all the details of the past three days—but I couldn't.

I didn't have the strength to speak.

We rode without saying a word. She gazed across the aisle enveloped in her thoughts as I stared at my bare feet. I needed to get rid of those pumps anyway. I was grateful for the distance from the week's chain of events and considered what would have happened had the bus driver listened to Mickey. I tried not to go there; the reality of my situation was overwhelming. Tortured and left dead in an empty warehouse, my bones dragged across the city by stray dogs. No one to pray for my soul. A cold shiver ran the length of my spine. The air was hot and heavy again, and I was freezing cold.

"Next stop," said the woman. She gently patted my hand. I would have cried had I not been afraid to draw more attention to myself. I obligingly left the bus from the rear exit. I blindly plodded along as we crossed street corners and down intersecting sidewalks. Passersby stepped aside affording *me* berth and girth.

I had become one of the street undesirables, another homeless person, obviously crazy. I thought of Charlie and his last location, a homestead for vagrants and gangs. The place where streetcar tracks were etched across a once baby soft face. The place where innocence was beaten to a pulp and replaced with blackened eyes and a darkened soul. I cried for Charlie. I cried for myself. I made wagers. I made the if-then deals with God, and I was ready to do the same with the devil if need be. If I could get out of this mess, I was going to help Charlie find a place to live, even if it meant sharing my living room sofa.

We climbed a steep, narrow set of metal stairs through a terraced backyard to the back of an apartment on a block of row houses. A cool breeze wafted through the shadowed walkway. We entered through a weathered door into a small apartment. It was a tight space but clean and quiet. Her apartment smelled like honeysuckle.

"Make yourself comfortable," she said, pointing to a sofa. "I'll make us some tea."

She was my junior by perhaps ten years, younger than I had first thought. Life's bumps and divots had left its mark. She had a round and full nose that balanced her high cheekbones and wide smile. She wore a faded tee shirt that hung loosely across her flat chest. Her jeans, rolled at the ankle, rode low on her bony hips. She kicked her flip-flops across the room and left me standing in the living room.

"I can't believe you helped me," I said, dropping my gaze to the floor. "You don't know me or what happened."

"Don't need to know you," she said, tugging the chain pull on the ceiling light in the kitchen.

Water whistled through the old pipes as she filled the teakettle. She held out a box of black tea. I nodded.

"I might have a little sugar."

"That's fine. I like it black," I said.

"See this," she said. She pulled her long twisted locks away from her neck. I gasped at the sight of a thick, ragged scar etched into her dark brown skin. "A man did this to me."

I paused in my response, waiting for the rest of her story. She didn't feel the need to explain, and I understood as I imagined her suffering.

"I'm humbled by your generosity. I'm also embarrassed to have lost my shoes."

"Can't help you with the shoes. Try these for now," she said, tossing me a pair of worn slippers.

"May I use your phone?"

"In the kitchen."

It was a small space with a two-burner stove, a small narrow refrigerator, and a wooden table for two covered with a faded plastic tablecloth and a vase of artificial flowers. There was a small counter with a chipped porcelain sink. I tapped on the side of the phone trying to remember the phone number for the precinct.

"Sorry, phone book?" I asked.

"In the drawer to your left," she shouted from the back of the apartment.

Swiping through the pages, I hurriedly searched for the number. I dialed from the mounted wall phone.

"I need to speak with Detective Hugo Gabby." The teakettle started to hum. "Harriet Crumford. I was kidnapped. They shot Charlie." I forced my dialogue; there was no time to wait for his response. "I don't know where I am. A nice lady has taken me to her house," I said. My voice quivered as I spoke just over a whisper.

"You believe me?"

His words resonated through my mind. They were the sweetest words I had ever heard.

"Mr. Woodard told you?"

I clutched the coiled telephone cord. "I'll ask."

I covered the mouthpiece with my hand. "What's the address here?" There was no answer. The teakettle whistled. "Hold on, Detective Gabby," I said. I dropped the phone and left it dangling against the wall. "Excuse me, what's the address here?"

I stopped short at the kitchen table.

The woman was sprawled on the living room floor.

Vic stepped into the doorway. Dried blood dotted the collar and front of his shirt. The gash on his cheek was wide and raw. His eye was puffy. The deep red veins along the side of his nose fed into a deep purple hue surrounding the gash. His mouth twisted toward the now favored side of his face.

Mickey put the phone to his ear before smashing it onto the cradle.

"She was on with Gabby."

"What did you do to her?" I shouted.

The teapot whistle screamed.

"Nothing a little nap won't fix," said Mickey.

I ran to the back door and fumbled with the lock.

Mickey shoved me to the side, grabbing me by the arm, twisting it behind my back. He pressed the side of my face against the wall.

"Going somewhere?" asked Vic, taking the kettle from the open flame. He spoke through a ridged and fixed jaw.

Vic ran his hand across the jagged edge of the raw and torn flesh across his cheek. He edged the tip of his hook into the open flame. I shook my head. Mickey tightened his grip and yanked my wrist toward my shoulder. It felt like my shoulder had been ripped clean from the socket.

"You're not going to like this," whispered Mickey as he covered my mouth. My knees buckled. I crumpled toward the floor. Mickey pulled me to my feet.

Vic brought the red-hot hook toward the side of my face. I tried to shake my head free. I screamed, kicked, and stomped. I tried to thrash free of Mickey's grip. He pressed an open hand against my throat. It hurt to breathe.

Vic pressed the hot metal to the side of my face. I screamed until I was lost of voice.

"That squares us," said Vic.

"This time you're going quietly," said Mickey, throwing me to the floor. "How about a blue diamond? All women like blue diamonds." He laughed as he forced a bitter blue tablet into my mouth.

"Say nightie-night!"

Chapter 24

"Wake up, Harriet!" screamed my mother. Her piercing voice pounded in my head.

"Go away," I said from a happy place of flashing lights, muted voices, and a wonderful tingling sensation. Weightless and free, I ran along a rose petal-covered garden path, chasing a twelve-foot butterfly for a kiss.

I skipped through the soft petals and followed the butterfly under a sage-colored gardenia, wondering why I hadn't planted this color in my garden, trying to make a mental note just as my senses skidded off to the side. Everything tingled. Rainbow-colored glitter rained from a cloudless sky. I was free. I *knew* I could fly.

"Hattie, wake up," repeated my mother. She kissed my cheek.

That stopped me in my tracks. A sign of affection and my mother called me, *Hattie*.

"I love you," she said, crying. "You have to wake up. *They're coming!*"

Somewhere from my mental stupor, I knew my mother was dead. I fought for reason and sensibilities to take hold.

I didn't want to wake.

I gave back into the blue diamond. I closed my eyes. I craved the dream.

"Harriet!" she screamed. "Hide!"

I awoke on a chair with drool trailing down my chin and a pounding headache. Pressing the back of my hand against my forehead, trying to right my senses. The savor of blue diamonds lingered between waves of hot flashes and clamminess. My cheek throbbed. It hurt to open my mouth. It hurt to swallow. I fought to lift my arm to read my watch. No watch. My limbs, heavy and sore.

I must have been out for hours.

Blue Diamonds.

The bittersweet tablet Mickey had forced into my mouth.

I wanted another. I wanted to go back to the butterfly.

I sat taking in my surroundings through slatted eyes.

It was a magnificent bedroom, heavy in gold trim and thick tapestries. The lights were out, the room comfortably balanced with natural light. The fireplace to my left was high enough for a full-grown man to stand. An ornately woven carpet with a scene of children playing among flowers filled the space from the chair to the fireplace. There was a massive four-poster bed with lavishly carved posts and headboard. There was a small desk, a large dresser, and bookcases that surrounded the fireplace. The bed was covered with a heavy spread and an overabundance of lush pillows; if only I could have detained myself in here under more pleasant circumstances.

Reality hit me square between the eyes as I cradled my aching head. From my drugged stupor, I pushed through the heavy fog. I eased to the edge of the chair and onto my feet. It hurt to stand. My feet were bruised, bloodied, and swollen. Somewhere, I had lost the donated slippers. I thought of the dear woman that risked her life to help me and wondered if she was still sprawled on her living room floor. Her only fault, underestimating my adversaries.

I listened at the door. Slowly, I turned the doorknob. The door was secured from the other side. I needed a weapon. I grabbed a rubber doorstop, hacking into thin air. Tossing it aside, I lifted a Bible from the nightstand. Barely able to swing it, I dropped it to the floor, I thought again, brushed it off, and gently set the Lord's words on a tufted pillow. The wall clock would do more damage to me than to my assailants. Forcing the heavy drapes to the side, I yanked the braided tieback from the wall, then tossed it to the floor. They would probably use it to choke the life out of me. I pleaded with the window to open. No neighbors. No gardeners. Just a well-groomed lawn and high fence. I searched through the drawers and around the shelving for anything to use as a weapon. The closet was empty.

I ran to the bathroom and stood frozen at the unfamiliar reflection of myself in the mirror. My hair was damp and matted around my ears and forehead. What little mascara I had on this morning was now a streaked mess that ran down my cheeks. Funny how the mind overlooks the obvious. I was busy checking out my dirty feet and messed hair, running makeup, and torn stockings while a hook-shaped branded blister was stamped across my left cheek. Branded. Branded by the man with the metal hand. Branded by someone without a soul.

I gently patted the blister. A portion of the skin was black from searing. The pain was unbearable. The surrounding skin around my cheek was taut and an angry shade of red. The constant throb superseded any other ailment plaguing my sore extremities. It hurt to move my mouth, my head, my neck, my knees, and my feet. My stockings were full of runs and torn at the toes. I pulled the cursed things off, tossed them into the small wastebasket, and leaned over the sink.

My face was a billboard advertisement of the improper way to live life. Eyes that once twinkled at possibilities were now nothing more than empty teacup saucers. I must have done something terrible somewhere along the way to deserve this karma. Looking at the folder? Being complacent with life? Not living to my full potential? Or just being in the wrong place at the wrong time. So many what-ifs flooded forward I thought I would have to flush them down the sink.

There was no time to waste on what-ifs.

There was only now, and *now* may only be but a moment.

I was on my own.

Tearing open the cabinet under the sink, I found a toilet scrubber, plunger, and a can of a bleachy bathroom cleaner. These would have to do.

I needed to hide, and quickly.

Ridiculous, I thought, to squeeze under the bed. I wagered my choices. Distance and aggravation. A toilet plunger and scrubber my only defenses. I pulled and squeezed under the edge of the bed with the plunger and scrubber, but found myself only partially wedged. Damn beignets!

Nowhere to hide behind the ancient carved wooden posts and thick canopies. I ran around the room, corner to corner.

Climbing into the claw-footed tub, I steadied myself with the spray can of bathroom cleaner and the toilet scrubber. I pulled the shower curtain closed and waited.

Every creak and groan of the building sounded like men's voices. My heart pounded in my chest, jarring my body with each beat. I closed my eyes. Tears rolled down my face, stinging my cheek.

Then, I heard them.

I knew this was it.

They were coming for me.

Stay focused. Stay calm. Wait for the opportunity. Don't force the moment.

I held my breath and listened as the door opened.

"She's gone!" I recognized the voice immediately. It was Mickey.

"Don't be ridiculous!" shouted Vic.

They were both in here.

I inhaled a long deliberate breath. My body shook. It made me sick thinking about being carried into the room with my skirt up around my neck, my panties exposed.

"You should have let me kill her last night when I had the chance. The bitch has been nothing but trouble."

I stood motionless in the tub, watching the shower curtain and waiting for a chance. The bathtub was shaking.

"This ain't no game of hide'n sneak," said Mickey.

"You idiot," said Vic. "It's hide *and seek*."

"Shut up, Vic," yelled Mickey.

"Come out from there," said Vic, drawing back the shower curtain.

Stay focused. Stay calm. Wait for the opportunity. Don't force the moment.

Mickey reached for me.

I smacked his hand with the dirty scrubber.

"You bitch!" shouted Mickey, tearing the shower curtain from the rod. "She hit me with a toilet scrubber. I'll make you eat it!"

I leaned away, pulling my girth toward the opposite side of the tub.

"I'll cut her up in a million pieces."

"You can't do that in here. This ain't your neighborhood. You'll have the cops breathing down our necks—not to mention Brizee," said Vic.

"I'm going to beat her to a pulp like I did to that dumb doorman," said Mickey.

My heart sank.

The doorman.

They had killed Rudy.

That's why he had missed our luncheon.

I almost dropped the scrubber.

"Where is he?" I asked.

Mickey's lips pulled back over his teeth as he smiled.

"Why would you kill him?"

Mickey winked. He was a soulless bastard. I wanted to cry for Rudy. I wanted to cry for Charlie. They were going to kill me, too. No one would ever know what had happened to the missing doorman of the Eldridge Building, the homeless man from the corner, and the crazy eighth-floor Harriet Crumford. All three, yanked from their notched place and space on the planet. Rudy had a mother to grieve and pray for his soul. Who would miss Charlie? Maybe Charlie had a family that checked in with him from time-to-time. Who would grieve for me? I didn't have a family. I didn't even have a cat. If I get out of this, I am getting a cat.

Everything has a time and place.

But this was not the time or place for grief or tears.

"Let me at her!" yelled Mickey. He darted toward me. Vic hooked his metal hand onto the sleeve of Mickey's shirt. Mickey smacked the hooked hand away.

"Stay away from me!" I yelled at the top of my lungs, hoping someone would hear. I squared my footing in the bottom of the tub.

"You're gonna suffer, bitch!" shouted Mickey, thrusting his knife toward me. His face was red. His eyes narrowed. The vein on the side of his forehead pulsated.

"You gotta problem, Mouse. A mother complex? Grandmother...."

"Shut up!" interrupted Mickey, cracking his knuckles. He stepped toe-to-toe with Vic. His nostrils flared. He squared his shoulders and stretched his stance.

Just pop him, Vic, I thought. That's what I needed. Let them get into a scuffle—just leave enough room for me to get to the door. I took a deep breath.

"Momma too rough on you?" continued Vic.

"Shut up." Mickey shoved Vic.

Vic stepped back. "Get her out of here," he ordered.

"I'm not going anywhere!" I scooted to the end of the tub, wielding the scrubber.

I readied the scrubber and aimed for the gash on his cheek.

"Was it as good for you as it was for me?" asked Vic. He held up his hook and smiled.

How dare he smile! How dare he rob me of my innocence. How dare he kill Rudy and *my* Charlie.

"You killed my friends!" I screamed. Rage filled every lost moment of my life. The kind of rage that makes nice old ladies lop off the heads of bad guys with a toilet scrubber.

I was fed-up with being pushed and shoved into compartments.

"You ruined my luncheon!" I screamed, swinging the scrubber. The words exploded from my mouth like buckshot from a shotgun on opening day. I swirled the scrubber over my shoulder like a bat.

"What the hell is she talking about?" asked Mickey.

"How was it to get a beating from an old woman? The two of you against one old woman," I said. "Such men! *Real* men do not harm and harass old women. Shame on you. Shame on your mothers for birthing such despicable excuses for human beings."

"You'll get out of that tub if I have to pull you out by the hair," said Vic.

"The police are on their way! Detective Gabby knows all about the blue diamonds. I'm wearing a tail in my skivvies," I said.

"What is she talking about?" asked Mickey. "What the hell is a skivvy?"

"She's a nut case," said Vic.

"Told you she was working with Gabby," said Mickey.

"He'll be here any minute with the swat team and the CIA."

"She's a lunatic!" shouted Mickey.

"Not to mention, Voodoo," I said, pulling my lips back exposing my teeth.

"I don't want any Voodoo shit, Vic," said Mickey. "It made my Gramps go crazy."

"Give me that thing!" shouted Vic, reaching for the scrubber.

I swung at him, scratching Mickey across the face. "I will not," I said, stepping to the other side of the tub.

"She hit me in the face with a toilet scrubber!" shouted Mickey, wiping the red lines etched across his face with the bottom of his tee shirt. He spit on the floor, then snarled, exposing his expanse of teeth. "I'm going to make her eat it."

"Brizee will take care of her," said Vic.

"She's been nothing but trouble," said Mickey. "I've had enough of this mess. When am I getting my money? I want a bigger cut for having to deal with this bitch! You never said anything about babysitting a lunatic. *Just* pass out the diamonds. Conjure business. Instant clientele, you said. *Easy* money."

"Shut up, Mouse," yelled Vic. His eyes narrowed. He looked hard at Mikey and then hard at me. I clung to the toilet scrubber and the spray can as I clung to my life. Vic motioned for me to exit the tub. I hugged the wall. Mickey leaned forward on the tips of his toes and reached for my blouse. Vic held him to the side. "You can't have her yet, Mouse. No commotion in *his* house."

Mickey grabbed for me anyway. I sprayed him in the eyes with the bleach cleaner. I held down the nozzle and sprayed the bleachy-foamy soap on the side of Vic's face. He buckled forward from the sting. Mickey pressed both palms to his eyes and yelled. I sprayed back and forth until the can emptied. I threw the can at Vic and hopped over the rim of the tub, tripping and landing on all fours. I crawled as fast as I could toward the door. Mickey caught me by the heel and pulled my leg out from under me. My forehead cracked against the marble floor. I rolled to my side and swung wildly, dragging the toilet scrubber across Mickey's face again. Wrestling myself to my feet, I slipped across the wet floor almost to the door.

Mickey slammed the door shut.

Vic held a knotted fist to the side of my head. His upper lip twitched. His splotched shirt smelled of bleach; an improvement I thought over his usual stale cigarette odor. Mickey twisted my arm behind my back and righted me to my feet.

They forced me along a wide hallway peppered with expansive wooden doors and raised wallpaper. It felt more like a hotel than a private home. We exited through a great room out onto a breezeway. I wasn't in a mansion. I was in the carriage house.

Mickey squeezed my arm. "Stop looking around, or I'll pop your eyeballs," he said.

We entered through the back door of a grand estate. Sculpted shrubs stood guard at the sides of a massive leaded-glass door. I walked with my head down following the black and white tiled flooring through an expansive kitchen. I heard the shuffling of feet but was afraid to look up, probably the kitchen staff leaving the area. I wondered if it was customary in this home for guests to be wrestled in through the back door.

This was not a kitchen like mine with wooden cupboards and a front and back door, welcoming all visitors to pass through of their own free will and volition. This was a house as cold as its stainless steel countertops and appliances.

I was shuffled down a long wood-paneled hallway to the center of the house. Wide double stairs joined from opposite wings of the second floor midway down to the main floor. A crystal chandelier, larger than my living room, shadowed across the marble floor with patterned blotches of dancing light. At the bottom of the stairs was a round table with a vase of fresh flowers. Eucalyptus and rose petals harshly toyed with my senses.

Unwillingly, I marched towards a double-doored room of rich wooden paneling, silver doorknobs, and shelves lined with books. Thickly framed oil paintings, yellow from time, adorned the walls. A woman sat with her back to us on an upholstered sofa. She spoke just above a whisper into a phone. Her stark blue-black hair hung neatly across the back of her neck and shoulders as though each strand had been individually placed. My heart raced at the sight of another woman.

Mickey pushed me from behind. I swung the scrubber. He jumped forward with a fisted hand. Vic stepped in front of him. Mickey wiped his face with the back of his hand. His piercing eyes spoke for him. The woman hung up the phone and turned.

I almost let go of the scrubber.

Dauphine Pascal.

I should have recognized her by the long lacquered nails and blue-black hair. She rose from the sofa, tugging her tight leather skirt down her thighs. She dismissed herself and acquiesced without saying a word. She gathered a small ostrich handbag and as gracefully as a dandelion in the wind, left the room.

No eye contact. No emotion. Not one shred of sorrow. I choked on my gullibility.

They forced me through a set of double doors into an office.

A white-haired man sat in an oversized leather chair with his hands folded across his lap. Dark sunglasses rested across the bridge of his sharp nose. Pockmarks fanned across his white panhandle-sandy colored cheeks. I dropped the scrubber. It was *him*.

It was the man with the sand dollar face.

I wished these were men looking for information about bedroom photographs. I wished they were importers and exporters of a rare commodity, like the diamond ring on Dauphine Pascal's finger.

They weren't.

They were ruthless, international, underground, gang-related traffickers of drugs—Blue Diamonds.

I wanted some.

Chapter 25

"What is that?" asked the man, pointing to the scrubber. His voice was loud and imposing, despite the fact that he looked frail and petit. His face was void of emotion. He was wearing a black silk dressing gown over a stiffly starched pointy-collared shirt and sweater. He sat on the corner of his desk, dangling his slippered foot.

In one swift motion, Mickey hiked the scrubber from the rug. "This bitch…."

"Your stench sickens me!" said the man with the sand dollar face. "What happened to your clothes?" He waved a finger at Vic and Mickey.

"Bathroom cleaner," said Vic, wiping at the splotched collar of his shirt.

"Why do the two of you insist on causing me distress?" asked the man. The corners of his mouth pointed down as harshly as the tips of his collar.

"It was her—she's crazy!" shouted Mickey.

"How dare you raise your voice to *me*!"

Vic drew in a long deep breath. I readied myself to run.

"How dare you allow your incompetency to flood my home? Why did you bring her *here*?" His crooked teeth were yellow, like his old paintings. It struck me odd that with all his money that he should have crooked and yellow teeth.

"There were witnesses," said Vic.

"So you bring her here?" The man stood and slammed his fist on the desk. "You leave a trail a child could follow right to *my* home. Perhaps you need another reminder, Monsieur Boudreau?"

From the corner of my eye, I caught a glimpse of Vic's metal hand as he quickly slid it into his pocket. "No, Monsieur Brizee."

Monsieur Brizee. Victor Boudreau. Mickey Mullen. Dauphine Pascal. They were all slaphappy with the name-dropping. There was no doubt in my mind…they would not let me go. My eyes trailed to Vic's pocket and back to the man with the sand dollar face. These people meant business.

The man motioned for me to take a seat. I folded my bare and dirty feet under the chair.

I was afraid to blink.

I was afraid to stare.

I was afraid to look away.

I was afraid to move and especially to breathe.

"You have caused me a great deal of trouble, Mrs. Crumford." His speech was precise and flowed as gracefully as his female assistant's gait. "You keep getting into my business. I do not like people in my business, Mrs. Crumford." His voice, piercing like his eyes. Purple blood filled the small veins around the side of his nose.

"What do you want from me?" I asked.

"I have the authorities breathing down my neck," he said, ignoring my question.

"I don't even know who any of you are," I said, waving my hand at Mickey and Vic.

"I don't like the police breathing down my neck. Do you understand, Mrs. Crumford?" He sat back down on the corner of the desk.

I swallowed hard past the growing lump in my throat. "I can't imagine what I have to do with it," I said.

"I don't like people taking from me!" he shouted, slamming his fist on his knee.

"You're going to kill me," I said in almost a whisper, fighting back the tears. I thought of Rudy and wondered if they sat him in this chair before they killed him. I checked the armrests for a sign, fingernail claw marks or blood—remnants from his tortured death.

"*I'm* not going to kill you," said Monsieur Brizee.

"What did you do to Rudy?"

"So, you do know something," said Brizee.

"I heard *them* talk about him," I said, nudging my shoulder in their direction.

Brizee glared at Vic who in turn looked at Mickey.

Vic rocked heel-to-toe staring at the carpet. "The doorman," he said, softly.

"*The doorman*," said Brizee.

"Oui, Monsieur."

"Take care of it!" shouted Brizee, waving his hands.

"Armondo…" Vic stepped forward.

Armondo Brizee. All the unraveling events tied in and around Armondo Brizee and his blue diamonds. The man with the sand dollar face.

"You dare question me?" asked Brizee.

Vic nodded. Mickey cracked his neck to the left and the right and pulled at the already stretched collar of his three-day-old tee shirt. "I'll send word to Crawdaddy to expect a couple of packages," said Mickey. "He's a true naturalist. Likes feeding the 'gators."

"Woodard?" asked Brizee.

"MIA," said Victor, holding the palm of his hand to his forehead.

Concern and contempt for Mr. Woodard sat heavily in my gut as he knowingly dragged me into this dangerous situation.

Armondo Brizee drummed his fingers on the top of his desk.

"Mrs. Crumford," shouted Brizee. I nearly jumped out of my skin. "You know something."

"I don't know anything."

"She's lying," said Mickey. "She knows about blue diamonds."

"He fed it to me!" I yelled.

Mickey backed up. Armondo Brizee's lips pressed together into a fine pink line across his white face.

"Start at the beginning." Armondo Brizee settled into his leather chair and folded his hands across his desk.

Vic stepped next to my chair and tucked his metal hand back into his pocket.

I wondered to what offense Monsieur Brizee offed the hands of his associates. I buried mine under my thighs.

"The beginning of...."

"Monday morning, Mrs. Crumford," interrupted Brizee.

I cleared my throat.

"Mickey, get Mrs. Crumford a glass of water," he instructed, pointing to a decanter of water on a side table.

Grumbling, Mickey forced the glass of water in my face.

"Could I have something stronger?" I asked.

"Stronger?" asked Mickey. He made a fist.

"My head is killing me. I haven't eaten all day. May I have a cup of tea with cream and sugar?"

"Mickey," instructed Brizee, "tell the kitchen to make a cup of strong tea for Mrs. Crumford."

"Don't forget the sugar," I said, pointing a finger at Mickey.

"I ain't her servant," interrupted Mickey. "I ain't waiting on her."

Brizee's face reddened.

Vic inhaled and held his breath. "Mouse," he whispered.

"Never mind," I interrupted, "I'll just have the water." Mickey held out the glass. I took a long sip. It hurt to move my mouth. Vic grabbed me by the back of my neck, already riddled with his fingerprints from the limo ride.

"Answer the question," instructed Vic.

"I went into the office Monday morning, as usual," I said, pausing for clarity. Rudy was dead. I would be next. This was not the time to invoke anger or solicit unnecessary questioning.

"But it wasn't usual?" said Brizee. He rested his elbow on the desk. This desk made Mr. Woodard's desk look like a child's toy. It was shiny as glass and as long as it was wide. I doubted there was a room in the whole of my house big enough for such an ornate piece of furniture.

"A man came in," I continued, "had a heart attack, and died on the office floor. I went for help, and his body disappeared." I shrugged my shoulders as if that was that and there was nothing more to it. I started to stand.

"Sit down," said Vic, slamming me back onto the chair.

"What was the man's name?" asked Brizee.

"I don't know. He didn't say."

"What's that? He didn't say?" Brizee pounded his fist on the desk. "What *did* he say?"

"The man said nothing. He died."

Brizee settled into the back of his chair as he traced the pock markings along the edge of his face. I didn't want to stare, but I couldn't look away. He kept running his fingers over and over the scars. "What did he say before he died?" he asked through clenched teeth.

"Nothing, he gasped for breath and died."

Brizee jumped to his feet. He snapped his fingers and pointed to me. Vic brought a handgun to my head. Brizee walked toward me. He grabbed onto the arms of my chair. I wanted to look away. His face was almost touching mine. His hand was touching my arm. Rudy had leaned against the same arm. Sweat covered Armondo Brizee's powder-white complexion. His snow-white eyebrows furrowed above his sunglasses. He smelled like my grandmother's spice rack. "You like looking at my face?" he asked.

"No reason to look or not look," I said.

Armondo Brizee removed his sunglasses.

I gasped at his white feather-like eyelashes.

"Mrs. Crumford, I am not a patient man." His pale blue eyes narrowed.

"Man with the sand dollar face. That's all he said."

"What else, Mrs. Crumford?" asked Brizee.

"He tried to whisper, but he died. The police didn't believe me." I laughed nervously. "A dead man getting up and leaving the office. I can't even believe it."

He smacked the back of my chair. "Where is he now?" asked Brizee, his glare at Vic unfaltering.

"He *is* dead."

"What did you do with the body?" yelled Brizee.

"We dumped him in an empty office."

"You idiots," he roared, "soiling my business with your game of chess."

Armondo Brizee rolled open a desk drawer and pulled out my purse. He set it on top of his desk. "What else?" he asked.

A cold chill ran down my spine. I felt like a child caught in a lie and pushed into a corner.

Brizee opened my purse and turned it upside down. The crumpled paper dropped to his desk. I could almost read the words from my chair. *Blue Diamonds*. "Mrs. Crumford, you have something that belongs to me!"

"I don't know what you're talking about." I ran my hand along the hemline of my skirt and thought of the disk I had left with Detective Gabby. My hands were cold and clammy. What had I done? I wrapped my fingers around the arms of the chair and held on for dear life. I can't tell Armondo Brizee I gave his disk to the police. He'd chop off my hands, my feet, and my head.

"My business associates are not fond of having their picture taken."

"Dauphine Pascal took the photographs."

"I need the disk."

"I don't have it," I said. That was not a lie. I did not have the disk.

"I want what's mine. I want my recipe."

"Recipe?"

It made absolutely no sense to me. What recipe?

Then it hit me. The recipe. The disk. Blue Diamonds. The exchange at the restaurant. It was a tangled mess.

At that moment I was sure I *hated* Mr. Woodard. Two people dead. My fate destined to be the same. Why didn't he mind his own business? Why did he have to get involved? He does matrimonial. No disks or recipes or killings with matrimonial investigations.

Brizee paced around the room. "Give Baxter a call. Tell him things have changed. We need a cleaning crew at the house. Bring the car around." Victor nodded. Brizee leaned onto the arms of my chair. I wanted to look away. He offered nothing more than a meaningless smile.

"Shut her up. I've got company coming. See to it that she doesn't go anywhere. After they've gone, take her for a ride. Get the location of that disk out of her! It goes tonight to the highest bidder."

They sandwiched me between the barrel of a gun and a knife.

Unwillingly, I followed.

They walked me to the service entrance through the back of the kitchen. Past the stainless steel countertops and appliances. Past the open shelving of pots and pans and the stocked pantry. My arms and legs weighed a ton as sluggish thoughts of me as alligator bait, and a trip in the bayou with Crawdaddy circled through my brain.

"Mickey, tie her up," said Vic, shoving me against the wall. The wall felt cold against my sweat-soaked blouse. Mickey pulled strips of latex tubing from his pocket. "You carry that shit around with you?"

"Never know when the opportunity might present itself. Loud-mouthed bitches are always pushing my buttons," said Mickey, pulling my hands behind my back.

"You are a sick bastard," said Vic.

Mickey drew his thick lips across his expanse of teeth into a smile. He tugged on my wrists.

"You're a psychopath," said Vic.

"How are you any different?" asked Mickey.

"I do what I have to. You do it for pleasure."

"Sounds the same to me," said Mickey.

"Tie her up and lock her in the closet. I'll grab the car," said Vic.

"Wait," I said, "is that latex? I'm allergic to latex."

"Shut up," said Mickey.

"I can't touch latex. I'll have a severe allergic reaction."

Mickey snapped my arm around to my back and shoved me into the wall. I winced from the pain of torn tissue. I thought my shoulder had popped out of the socket. He wrapped the latex tubing around my wrist.

"Give me your other hand!" He pulled my wrist up toward the back of my head. "You fat pig!" he shouted. "Can't even get your hands around your back?"

Mickey forced my other arm back. He pulled my wrist. I sank toward the floor; I thought I would pass out. The pain was unbearable. He grabbed my blouse at the sleeve and violently swung me around, slamming the back of my head against the wall. His blackened eyes narrowed. I turned my head away from his breath. He forced my hands to my breasts, wrapping and knotting the latex tubing around my wrists. He wrapped another strip of banding around my mouth. The latex tubing cut into the sides of my mouth and across my blistered cheek. Tears freely flowed. He pulled the banding tighter. I made a guttural cry.

"Thanks for the quarters," he said, pushing me onto the hard closet floor. My face smacked against the ceramic tiles.

Chapter 26

The door slammed shut, suffocating me in darkness. I wrestled to my feet and grabbed for the handle. The knob would not turn. My throat felt thick as the familiar wheeze rattled in my chest. Death by latex would be kinder than death at the end of a gun barrel or as an alligator's appetizer. I wiggled my fingers; they were starting to swell. Dropping to the floor, I struggled for breath. I gasped for stale air among the jackets and aprons. Jackets? Of course! People leave things in their pockets. Keys, pocketknives—and in this house, maybe a handgun.

I felt around the small space. An umbrella. A pair of men's boots stuffed in the corner. I slid in my feet. I found what felt to be a silk scarf laden with the familiar scent of Lily of the Valley. I choked at the thought of touching what might belong to Dauphine Pascal, but I wrapped it around my neck anyway. I would take a piece of her with me to the grave. I felt through pockets and along the top shelving. Nothing.

It was hopeless.

I slid down the wall and landed on my rump. I rested my head against the wall seeking the cool solace as I faced the end of my life.

I tapped my head against the wall. Tap…tap…tap like the ticking of my missing watch. Tap…tap…tap like the turning signal on the bus. Tap…tap…tap…. Click clack.

The door unlocked.

I fumbled for the umbrella. The light switch clicked on. A young woman in a housekeeping uniform gasped. I held my hands out to her. I groaned between raspy breaths, motioning to the banding. I pleaded with my eyes.

She untied the banding from around my mouth and then my hands.

No time to thank her for saving my life.

Muffled voices of men gathered near the back entrance echoed through the sterile kitchen. I tore from the closet and down a narrow hall.

I had to find a phone.

I continued down the corridor to a small side bedroom. Slowly, I turned the knob and prayed for safe access. I gently coaxed the door open, scanning the room for occupants or possible shelter. They would be coming for me. They would tear through every closet and corner of this building until they found me.

I ran to the phone on the nightstand. What was Gabby's number? I tried dialing and got a wrong number. I tried again. My hands looked like balloons with fingers, my face so swollen I could barely see. I dialed 9-1-1.

"Call Detective Hugo Gabby," I whispered through a raspy voice, "334 Royal. I don't know where I am. I've been kidnapped. Hattie Crumford."

I dropped next to the bed and brought the phone to the floor. I waited.

I knew Mickey and Vic would come. They had no choice. Find me or face the wrath of Armondo Brizee.

They would find me before Gabby.

I sat and waited. Time ticked aimlessly. I was not eager to leave the planet. I didn't have any burning desires to join Eddie or my mother. After all, I had just gotten away from them. The thought of an eternity in the space of their company *would* be hell. I wanted strolls on the sidewalk. I wanted my bed and what semblance I held of life with peace and serenity. Knowledge of which cupboards held cups and which had the saucers. I wanted to live.

The door opened.

Mickey was all but frothing at the mouth as he circled the foot of the bed to my hiding spot.

I knew it would be him.

"I'll take that," he said, reaching for the phone.

I pulled the phone away from his grasp.

"Give me the phone," he said through clenched teeth. Then he spit on me; a glob of disgustingness and foulness clung to the side of my face.

"Okay," I said, giving him one solid clonk against the side of his jaw with the phone. He folded to the floor, out cold.

With swollen fingers, I searched his pockets. I ran down the hall and out a side door with Mickey Mullen's knife and car keys.

Fresh air filled my lungs. I ran across the manicured lawn and hid in the landscaped shrubbery. The house was enormous; four floors and two main wings that fed into a central space. The gardens, fenced with tall metal posts peaked and pointed.

I stood face to face with the impossible as I crouched in the bushes. I was not ready to die. I had lived with my life on hold. Holding onto values and principles that were not my own. I allowed myself to be told what to do and where to go. Where to put the cups, saucers, and bowls. The way to dress, the way to act. Taught to live according to the considerations of others. Then it hit me. It hit me hard. It wasn't their fault, Eddie or my mother.

It was mine.

I had allowed it. I had encouraged it by not speaking up. It was easier to put up with it than to face conflict. Easier to *never* fail if I lived without challenges.

The police would not find me in time—but the man with the sand dollar face would. Armondo Brizee wanted something from me like everyone else. He wanted *my* life.

I cannot give what I do not have.

I prayed for strength.

These men knew nothing of my life. They knew nothing of the flowers I had smelled or the paths I had walked. They knew nothing of a mother's heartsick suffering for the children she will never bear. They knew nothing of gratitude for second chances or anything else for that matter. Greed and violence were at the core of their existence.

If Mickey's car was there, I would find it. I ran toward the driveway.

I circled the row of limos and shiny black cars around to the side of the service entrance. There it was. It had to be. The car was as dirty and worn as Mickey's three-day-old stretched shirt.

I pulled open the door, catching a glimpse of a crumpled body on the floor of the back seat. I panicked and screamed.

It was Rudy.

Unrecognizable—except for his uniform.

His face, swollen. Mickey's favorite latex banding, tied around Rudy's wrists and ankles.

I was on autopilot, unwrapping the binding. "Oh, my dear, sweet Rudy, what have they done to you?" I cried, stroking his hair.

Then, my gut screamed to *get out of there*!

I jumped in behind the wheel.

I revved the engine as Vic and Mickey sprinted from the house and across the lawn. If I wanted to live, I would have to drive. I raced the car across the well-maintained lawn and over plantings.

"Rudy, if you can hear me…hang on the best that you can!" I screamed.

I floored the gas pedal and aimed the car at the gate. This was a one-way ticket out. I hit the fence full force.

Chapter 27

I awoke to Detective Gabby holding my hand. I thought I was dead or caught in another blue diamond dream. I tried to sit. He gently forced me back down on the bed. I raised a wrapped hand to my bandaged face. Everything hurt. It felt like ants and spiders were crawling under and over my skin. I wanted to scratch my skin raw. I wanted Blue Diamonds.

"Good news—nothing is broken," said Detective Gabby, smiling.

"My face?" I asked through clenched teeth.

"Going to be as beautiful as ever. Doctors said you should be ready for the runway next year." Detective Gabby smiled again.

"What about—."

"Barely noticeable. Doctors will talk to you about plastic surgery in a couple of days. What exactly were you thinking? Driving into the gate like that!" he asked. He fussed with the railing on the side of my bed.

"I saw it in a movie," I said.

He laughed. "I thought you didn't have a television," said Gabby.

"I didn't say I didn't go to the movies." I wanted to laugh, but everything hurt.

"Rudy's going to be okay. Beaten pretty badly. Two broken legs. Docs say he's going to pull through."

"They broke his legs?" Tears welled in my eyes.

"Hattie, you did when you tried to drive through the gate."

I let my eyes close. *The gate*, I thought.

"It's a wonder you didn't kill yourself."

"It was the only way for you to find me." I wanted to shift the weight from my sore hip, but I couldn't move. It felt like the mattress had swallowed me alive. "Thank you."

"You can thank Woodard. He gave us a lot to go on."

"Mickey Mullen and Vic?"

"Mickey's in jail."

Detective Gabby squeezed my hand. I started to cry.

"Vic got away," he said.

I tried to sit up. I wanted to run.

Detective Gabby pressed me back against the bed.

"You're going to be okay," he said. "I have an officer guarding your door. No one's going to hurt you."

"Armondo Brizee?" I asked.

"Got away in his helicopter," said Detective Gabby. "He's got dirty hands that extend far and wide."

The man with the sand dollar face would find me. I knew it. I had something he wanted...my life.

"I have a lot to tell you," I said.

"You get some rest first. I'm going to need you at your best if we're going to solve this case."

He handed me the television remote. "I thought you might like to try it out. We put together a few bucks down at the Precinct to buy you a television so you can watch the shopping network while you're recovering at home. I'll have one of my guys deliver it."

"I don't know how to thank you."

"It's not much."

"What about the woman who helped me?"

"She's fine. Bump on the head. She's been here a couple of times to sit with you."

Tears drifted down my cheek. I was alive. Rudy was alive. We were both going to have a second chance at life. I was not going to waste it. I was not going to blame someone else for missed moments.

"Detective Gabby, they drugged me."

"I know."

"I don't feel very good."

"You're coming down off the blue diamond. A new designer drug. More addictive than heroin, and more deadly," explained Detective Gabby. "You helped keep it off the streets. Well, for now anyway."

"Am I an addict?" I asked. My eyes filled with tears.

Detective Gabby's glance to the floor was answer enough.

"The dead man was an informant," I said.

"Found his body," said the detective. He walked to the end of my bed.

"Mr. Woodard?"

"Laying low for a while. That's enough shoptalk for now. You need to rest. Are you up for a little company? There's someone here to see you—been here nonstop for days."

"Who?"

Detective Gabby ushered in a clean-shaven man I recognized from somewhere.

"Charlie!" I shouted. *My* Charlie.

He leaned over the bed and kissed me on the forehead. His wrist bandaged, his arm in a sling.

"I heard the second shot. I thought…."

"Miss Hattie, I'm not homeless. I'm undercover, well, at least I was until this," he said, pointing to his wrist. "I had to blow my cover when you came barreling past me. I couldn't catch up; I was bleeding too much. By the time help came, you had disappeared. I'm sorry."

"Undercover?" I couldn't stop looking at him…my Charlie. Not homeless. "Charlie." That was all I could say.

"I've been watching those two for a month. Nothing more than two-bit cons and petty criminals until they got hooked up with Brizee. He had them scattering blue diamonds on the streets until Woodard stumbled in on the exchange. The dead man in your office was one of our informants. He went to your office to warn Woodard. It seems Woodard somehow got his hands on half of the formula. That's what was on the disk."

"Miss Hattie, there's someone I want you to meet." Charlie opened the door for a young woman carrying a chubby baby girl with pink cheeks and soft dark curls. "Miss Hattie, this is my wife, Becca." The woman pressed against the side of my bed. She smelled of lilies and baby powder.

"I'm so honored to meet you, Miss Hattie," said Becca. She squeezed my hand.

"Miss Hattie, I'd like to introduce you to our daughter," said Charlie. "Her name is *Hattie*."

"Hattie?" I whispered. "You named her Hattie?"
"Yes ma'am, after you, her new Meemaw."

Sometimes the best place for the cups *is* near the saucers.